Lou Andreas Salomé
Ruth: A Tale

1895

Translated By Carl Hermesson 2024

© 2024 by Carl Hermesson. All rights reserved.

This translation of a public domain work is protected under copyright law. While the original work is not subject to copyright restrictions, this translation is a unique interpretation.

Contents

Translators Preface......... 5
I.. 7
II... 50
III. 93
IV. 126
V. 173
VI. 214

Dedicated to Muschka

Translators Preface

"Ruth" is a masterful exploration of human emotions and relationships set against the backdrop of early 20th-century Russia. This narrative, rich in psychological depth and social commentary, traces the lives of Erik, Ruth, and the intricate web of connections that bind them. The story delves into themes of love, duty, and the existential struggles that define the human experience.

Lou Andreas-Salomé was born on February 12, 1861, in St. Petersburg, Russia, into a family that combined French Huguenot and German heritage. Her father was a Russian army general, and her mother was a German of French descent. She was identified as a child genius at an early age and her circumstance made her able to develop this disposition into Ruth and many other masterful works of literature.

Salomé's intellectual journey began in earnest when she moved to Zürich at the age of 21, one of the few places at the time that offered higher education to women. She studied philosophy and theology, disciplines that would deeply influence her later work. Her quest for intellectual and personal freedom took her to Germany, where she became an influential figure in the literary and philosophical circles.

Her life was marked by her relationships with some of the most prominent thinkers of her era. Friedrich Nietzsche, Sigmund Freud, and Rainer Maria Rilke were among her closest friends and intellectual companions. Nietzsche proposed to her, but she declined, choosing instead to pursue her intellectual passions independently. Her friendship with Freud led to her significant contributions to psychoanalysis, and her relationship with Rilke inspired some of his most profound poetry.

Andreas-Salomé was not only a novelist but also a philosopher, psychoanalyst, and essayist. Her works explore themes of love, sexuality, and the human psyche with a depth and clarity that were ahead of her time. Her life and work continue to inspire and challenge readers and scholars, cementing her legacy as one of the most intriguing and insightful figures of her time.

- Carl Hermesson, Berlin 2024

I.

In the morning stillness, nothing was audible except the bright, prolonged trilling of the little chaffinches in the young birch leaves. The wide, unpaved road, stretching out into the flat countryside not far from the Russian capital, near the Finnish railway line, lay lonely in the early mist. Then, a cart laden with some pieces of furniture clattered heavily along the way; the driver climbed down from his seat, threw off his short sheepskin coat, and, in his red shirt, walking beside his lean horses, began to sing a folk song that melancholically blended with the birds' song.

Behind the birches, a country house occasionally appeared, mostly wooden structures with closed shutters and boarded-up balcony doors; or a garden glimmered, where people were busily gathering the winter leaves and preparing the beds for summer. But it didn't come alive in this area until after the start of the city's school holidays.

The furniture cart stopped in front of a house, which lay quite isolated, far from any neighbors, amidst low willow bushes and somewhat damp meadow ground. It was not particularly large but had the best garden of all. The spring trees surrounding it spread a delicate brownish veil over it, and all around the weathered wooden fence, lilacs with light green leaf buds clustered.

"Push the gate open from the outside!" a cheerful voice called out in broken Russian to the driver, and immediately afterwards, a teenage boy came running through the garden. Slowly, the cart moved over the gravel to the back of the house, where a few steps led up to the open terrace with the entrance door.

An elderly maid, wearing a peculiar Frisian cap on her head, was already waiting below, helping energetically and letting the unloaded pieces of furniture be set down in the living room, which with its wide window looked out onto the terrace. In the living room, the door to a smaller adjoining room was open, which seemed to be already fully furnished. From the items found upon moving out of the city apartment into the rented country house, evidently, all the best and most comfortable things had been gathered here to create order and coziness.

On a blanket-covered daybed by the door lay a pale, no longer young woman, whose fine facial features still showed traces of unusual former beauty. Under her half-lowered eyelids, she attentively followed every movement of those coming and going.

Then, from the terrace, she heard a voice that brought a smile to her large blue eyes.

"Erik!" she called pleadingly, "come here to me. Please come."

He stood by the terrace window, in a dark morning jacket, his hands in his side pockets, a cigarette between his teeth. At his wife's call, he turned and went into the room.

To her, it always seemed as if a stream of life came with him when he approached her like this.

"Well, Bel," he said cheerfully, "you'll see, the sun will break through the mist now, and then I'll carry you out into the garden. We've already set up your large reclining chair by the fountain back there."

She shook her head.

"I can't rest outside as long as everything here is still in such a mess. How might it look in your rooms, Erik? Since we arrived yesterday, you've only taken care of me. Oh, you know, that's the worst: in the whole of life, nothing will ever be properly in order again. Everything will lie around."

"But, Bel!" he replied mockingly, "what sense would it make to tidy up otherwise? What worries and pains these are!"

But Klare-Bel did not join in the joking tone and instead looked sadly in front of her. He added impatiently, "You must come to terms with it seriously. Don't keep bringing it up. Surely, you were meant to be the most meticulous of housewives sitting behind the shiniest of all tea machines, and now you have to lie there year after year and watch helplessly as your two male housewives, Jonas and I, carelessly handle things. It's hard, I know. It's hard to suppress your talent. But you can't avoid it; you must finally overcome it."

"Jonas could almost be like a daughter to me, Erik, if you only wanted."

"That he would be like a daughter? No, of course I don't want that. How can you talk such nonsense, Bel."

"It's not nonsense, Erik. You are so strict with him, and that's why he is often shy around you, doesn't open up fully. But serving me gives him joy – even in domestic matters. Can't you leave me this joy?"

"No," he said shortly, "not in the way you mean it. It's my place to serve you –"

He broke off because the maid entered; she wanted to settle the bill with the driver.

Erik placed money on the table, which had been set in the middle of the room, still dusty.

"This is the tip, Gonne. No need to give back change. It's little enough for a lot of work."

When she had gone out, he looked at his wallet with a suppressed smile and then over at his wife.

"We have an awful lot of money, Bel. Naturally. Who should take it from us in this corner. Right?"

"Oh, Erik, that can't be. In this 'corner,' we've chosen one of the most expensive country houses. I didn't dare to object. But if you knew how it silently weighs on me. Because you are the one who has to use all your strength to earn all that money."

"Using all my strength!" he repeated slowly, "how unfortunate, Bel, that it's not true. I almost think it would be so beautiful that I'd do it even for free! Then, of course, it wouldn't stop at those few miserable school hours. – No, you, in this holy land, I soon forget that I have to exert any strength at all. And then we should at least enjoy life when – I have money. Didn't we come here just for that, half a year ago?"

She didn't hear the irony in his tone.

"Well, Erik, it's just good that everything always seems too easy and too little for you," she said, "you have such a remarkable freshness. But I really don't know where, with the best will, you could squeeze in even more school hours?"

A trace of pain crossed his face. He didn't answer, but turned away and leaned into the wide window of the living room. Jonas had come in from the garden, stood beside his father, and looked out.

Outside, the last mist fought against the May sun; in the depth of the garden, one could distinguish individual groups of fruit trees, in the middle of which stood a collapsed fountain. In the background, a small grove of birches, poplars, and willows, still hanging with catkins, closed off the view. Closer to the house, a few mighty elms stretched their branches over the roof.

Sweet and loud, the first nightingale of the year sang to the two at the window. For a moment, they listened silently.

As the faces of father and son were so close together, their resemblance became noticeable; it was even more pronounced because Erik was clean-shaven. The same blond head, broad in forehead and skull shape, the same slightly blunt nose, and the same large mouth, very expressive in speech and laughter. But these somewhat coarse features clearly needed many decades to become spiritualized and captivating. Erik's features had become eloquent with all those fine lines and shadows that gave them a soulful charm only as youth left him. Jonas, on the other hand, still had a fresh apple face, which in its complete innocence often made him appear less alert than he really was. Only his large blue eyes, like his mother's, could be called beautiful, along with her dazzling skin, which had only been faded by the sickbed.

Klare-Bel lay still and looked at her two dearest people. In her thoughts, she already saw Jonas grown to the tall figure of her husband; she believed to see him in the boy as he had been when she first met him and he courted her. After all, there weren't so many years that separated him from Jonas' age at that time – Erik was only twenty-one when his son was born. She always felt a small surge of pride when she thought of it. He had been crazy enough in love with her to marry her right in the middle of his carefree Paris student days! He, the gifted, ambitious, early worldly man, bound himself to her, the simple governess, who had only been brought to the refined social circles of Paris by the lucky chance of a favorable position from her small Dutch hometown Haarlem. Holding the foreign children by the hand, she had admiredly peeked into the salon where he mingled. Later they moved from Paris to Germany and to England and lived for a few years on the small fortune that was quickly used up. Erik's studies had been broadly laid out, meant to encompass both humanities and natural sciences equally, but when Jonas was two years old, it was necessary to concentrate and complete them with iron diligence to earn a living. A small teaching position offered itself to him, quite out of the world, far out in the sea on a Frisian island. Klare-Bel was secretly happy that their crazy, happy student marriage ended in such quiet, orderly circumstances, but she felt sorry for Erik. For first, he was certainly destined for much greater things than this dependent quiet life for wife and child, and then she couldn't imagine him other than in the immense framework of a world city and in full interaction with a cultured, refined society that swept him along and that he swept along. When she first saw him among the simple people of the village, he seemed to her like an enchanted prince.

But she knew him and did not doubt: somehow he would enchant the people too, until they better suited his princely demands.

To her surprise, however, it turned out quite differently. Erik did not teach others his way, but rather adopted theirs. Soon, he was seen as often in a fisherman's jacket and leather pants as in his former clothes. His surroundings influenced him so strongly that he appeared completely authentic in the color. But the result was that he dominated his surroundings. He didn't give himself over to brooding about his far-reaching, ambitious desires, as Bel had feared; perhaps he was too active a nature for that.

He gathered everything he could to be fully active in the present, and in the future – he believed in it as firmly as a child believes in God.

Klare-Bel propped herself a bit higher on her pillows and supported her head with her hand. She never thought further than this.

A glow of happy memory lay on her face, rejuvenating it. The artfully arranged curls that framed her face instead of any fixed hairstyle still bore the same wonderfully pretty golden color as back then. Only at the back of her head had they become thin from the long lying, yes, there had even formed a tiny hidden bald spot.

"Now we have to go to school, Jonas," remarked Erik, turning away from the window.

"Are you going to the girls today, Papa?" asked he, interested.

"Yes. But you don't have to wait for me at the gate of the girls' school again and loiter around," replied Erik with a side glance that made Jonas embarrassed. Without a word, he trundled out of the room.

"Jonas is starting early! He's following in your footsteps, Erik!" said Klare-Bel with a smile, and as if her words were in some mental connection, she reached among various things on a low table next to her daybed and pulled out an opened letter. "Here is the invitation. If you really want to decline, don't forget to do so in the city today, or will you do it in person?"

He reached for the letter and glanced over it quickly. It was a short invitation, signed: Warwara Michailowna. Erik distractedly folded the paper into small creases and threw it back on the table.

"I'd like to ask you something, Erik."

"Yes, Bel?"

"Tell me: don't you go into that whole circle anymore because it has become dangerous for you?"

He began to laugh.

"No, Bel, you can be at ease about that."

"But didn't it captivate you quite strongly for a moment?"

"Indeed it did. That succeeds for every charming coquettish woman."

"Young widows are always considered coquettish. I wouldn't think that of Warwara. Do you believe that about her?"

He looked at his wife in surprise.

"Yes, of course. All beautiful women are. Nor is there the slightest reproach to make about it. It's part of them, like beauty. The opposite would almost be out of character. – And it's good – maybe a reason why beauty doesn't cause deeper harm. Goodbye, Bel; it's time for us to go to the station."

She held her face up for a kiss. But as he bent down to her, she wrapped her arms around his neck and held him for a moment, looking up at him.

He stood patiently still.

"You!" she said with a laughing mouth, let herself be kissed, and let him go.

Erik and Jonas had already left, and Gonne was eagerly and noisily tidying up the rooms when Klare-Bel still pondered the last conversation. She was truly not inclined to brood and muse, anything but. But if you had to lie still like that forever, always on your back, your eyes on the whitewashed ceiling, you eventually thought of all sorts of things, including thinking. Klare-Bel never really thought about herself, only indirectly. She fundamentally only had three serious, so to speak, main thoughts that required concentration: Erik, Jonas, and the dreaded disorder in the household. But it was remarkable how much you could make of these three if you combined them skillfully. You might think there were a thousand.

So, Erik had said earlier: beauty causes no deeper harm. Yes, that was certainly a real blessing. For Erik was very receptive to beauty. Already when she walked around healthy, it unsettled her. Fortunately, she was very beautiful herself, but she was blonde, and it seemed to her that the brunettes also interested him. Surely, he had fallen in love countless times. But only once did she startle, – truly started from all previous joy. During the second year on the island. Then he began to leave her alone so much; sometimes it seemed to her as if she no longer satisfied him as before. He also became more taciturn. And finally – yes finally she did what he should never know in his life: she followed him secretly.

It was on a soft, dark April evening. The sea lay motionless, and the first spring thunderstorm stood in the sky. She saw him come out of a small house, right by the dune, and walk home past her, lost in thought. In that house lived the most remarkable woman on the whole island. She was held in high esteem by all for her intellect, her demeanor in difficult and changeable fates, and for a rare treasure of wisdom and experience, from which she drew when a fine, loving connoisseur of people brought her to speak.

It was Mrs. Larsen, a lame sixty-year-old woman.

Since that evening, Klare-Bel had an unlimited trust in her husband.

•

Erik spent the first morning hours with Jonas in his gymnasium; around noon, he went to the large main school for girls, which was quite far away.

He had boarded a passing horse tram, and at one of the last stops, a colleague joined him. He looked overheated, kept his hat in his hands after the greeting, and fanned himself with his handkerchief.

"How are you, Mr. Matthieux?" he asked Erik, panting, "here in the city, May is already unbearable, – really, – at least when walking. And you don't dare to take off the summer coat; you expect an icy gust of wind from the Neva at any moment. Without transitions, without normal temperature. A murderous climate."

He accompanied his words with so many gestures that one got the impression he would never cool down in his life. Erik glanced quickly at the man sitting opposite him, of roughly the same age, on whose exposed, already heavily thinned hair the bright May sun shone mockingly from outside.

"Is that my future here? – May is unbearable!" he thought and said aloud: "I must confess, I have a weakness for this Russian spring. It may be naughty, perhaps more capricious and dangerous than any other, but for that, it is a wonder. It lingers so long, and then comes so unexpectedly and so unbelievably beautiful that you can't believe your eyes."

"Yes, yes. If one can keep eyes for it. I always go back to Germany after school ends and recover from the Russian gusts and conditions. I write a work – always during the holidays in Germany. That's my relaxation. So there's little left for the summer. That's how it is for all of us – all of us who have to overwork mentally."

Erik was silent for a moment, then replied, as if finishing a silent thought, calmly: "I see myself, admittedly, only very partially as an 'intellectual worker.'"

"Oh, you don't mean because you were over there, – because you spent a little too long in rural conditions –? but I beg you, with your knowledge and talent! Why shouldn't you write a work too?"

Erik laughed.

"No, that's not what I meant. Not that I might be a bit rustic from over there. Not the lack of books. Because we – the teacher above all – work mainly with human material. We belong somewhat outside the scholar's study, it seems to me. Right in the middle of life."

"Hm!" the colleague said, "I find you only come very superficially close to people. It really only remains desk work. But tell me: people talked about you wanting to give a series of lectures a few months ago? What happened with that?"

Erik's eyes darkened.

"Nothing happened with that!" he said shortly, "they denied me the hall!"

"You see, you see! That comes from your inconvenient view of the teaching profession outside the study. They fear you might become a bit lively. We all walk here with tied hands, – you know that! But you should really console yourself with one thing: there are simply no people here among whom anything could ignite and have an effect. There is only the people, to whom we are neither allowed nor able to speak, – and an audience that wants to be entertained."

He had gotten into a fervor. Erik did not reply. The horse tram stopped, and both got off.

"So, you have taken on new hours at the girls' school?" his companion resumed the conversation, and as he now walked slowly, fixing the pavement with his glasses, he looked as heavy and sleepy as he had been hurried and distracted before, "yes, they would like to use you for everything! You only had to take over this class in the fall."

"But there was a shortage of teachers. Also, I wanted to get to know the girls, make contact, before I take them over completely in the fall."

"Well, you'll get tired of it. You know, this gender is terrible! And not the slightest talent for mathematics among them. Not the slightest. They all can't calculate."

"Thank God!" said Erik.

"No, don't take it humorously. As a girls' teacher, you unlearn laughing. Surely, you don't like the adolescents in your class?"

"Hübsche Mädels!" Erik almost said; but when he saw his companion's almost worried expression, he bit his tongue in time and only said: "They do bring inspiration, variety. See, here in my leather case: a whole stack of essay notebooks. The most curious stuff. They still go back to my predecessor; I had them given to me only to get an orientation. I also found a real curiosity among them."

"I'm not curious about that!" the mathematics colleague assured, squinting his eyes, "truly not. But you are an enviable person. I know from your predecessor that these blue essay notebooks sometimes gave him nightmares even at night."

"That was just a fair punishment!" Erik laughed as they passed through a high archway and entered the school building, "why did he give essay topics like, for example, the last one here: 'On Happiness.' Poor girls, who are supposed to describe in beautiful German what they haven't yet enjoyed."

They stopped in front of the wide stone staircase leading from the hall to the classes.

"So, goodbye then!"

"Best of 'inspiration' wishes."

Erik climbed up and walked through the high hall corridor where the classrooms were. He opened one of them and looked at his watch. The breakfast break was not yet over. Most of the girls had been lured out into the large schoolyard by the May sunshine; through the open window, one could see them walking and playing in pairs below. Right under the window where he sat, there was a fountain with a wooden bench; there, a group of half-grown girls made themselves comfortable – the giggling and chatting clearly reached Erik up above.

In the surrounding classes and in the hallway, it was quite still; rarely did a door slam, or a call sound. The sun brooded over the half-lowered window blinds, and a few bumblebees buzzed around some bread crumbs on the dusty desks.

Erik had pulled out the blue notebooks and was leafing through them, occasionally letting out a sigh. Fundamentally, these were really quite boring school notebooks. Such an adolescent is interesting, without a doubt, interesting as a person, as a woman, as an adolescent, and a world in itself; but none of that comes into the school essay. No wonder! Isn't it ultimately the same with all written books in the world? Isn't the smallest slice of real life a thousand times richer, more revealing?

He stood up and cast a glance at the laughing, chatting group of girls by the fountain. Those he could see from his vantage point certainly belonged to his new class and were therefore responsible for the boring essays. He forgave them while looking at them – these fresh creatures, who still had the privilege of being beautiful without beauty. Among them, very distinct types were easy to distinguish, although they belonged to different nationalities. Three languages buzzed around. He could most clearly distinguish the more domestic and the more worldly type. Both had something appealing – both the mischievous look that peeked so femininely knowing under the carefully curled bangs, and the gentle, modest gaze under the Madonna parting. The truly childish genre was almost not represented among these adolescents. And perhaps for that reason, so little atypical, so little individual – they could already be classified, they were already firmly shaped by the environment in which they were raised, where there were no born educators and people-fishers according to Erik's ideal, but only ordinary officials and dignitaries.

Unconsciously, his hand searched among the notebooks, as if he wanted to prove himself wrong. Yes, here was the "curiosity" among the essays – something very individual indeed.

Instead of the prescribed title "On Happiness," it bore the heading "Blessedness!" – and something like a longing and jubilation sounded from this heading in every line. It was not written in reasonable, or at least correctable prose, but in verses, in completely uncorrectable and wild verses, in which language had taken flight. Nevertheless, these verses had an effect, however faulty they were written. Or rather: dreamed. For fundamentally, this resembled an unclear dream, a mere stammering of thoughts, a rebellion against words and logic, but it undeniably contained an emotional power. One became extremely impatient while reading, but was also overwhelmed by an impatient desire to force the dreamer and stammerer to give a clear account of their soul. Such verses might have been written by Saint Teresa as a child, before she related her visions to God, thought Erik. Which of those in the yard might it be?

Individual words sounded loud and excited up to him, interrupting his reading. He heard one of the girls' voices say with great energy: "He must be unhappy. I want it so. As unhappy as possible. Otherwise, I won't do it."

"No, no, I'm completely against that!" another cried sympathetically.

"Oh, I would agree," a third tried to mediate, "if it's only for a while. Because later, she marries him for it."

"Marries?" the first voice asked in astonishment, "no, I don't think of that! He remains and stays unhappy, I tell you. Once and for all. But I won't marry him."

Erik dropped the notebook. He leaned on the windowsill and looked down carefully. He wanted to know what the cruel creature looked like that wanted to torment the unfortunate one for life and not even marry him.

But she was evidently sitting right by the house wall and was surrounded by the others in such a way that Erik couldn't lean further down without being seen from below. He only saw two narrow, far-stretched feet in cut-out shoes and dark stockings.

Now they all twittered so loudly that nothing could be understood.

Then a very pretty dark-haired adolescent said, while heartily biting into an apple: "I really find it funny of you. Because what else did we stuff him with so many and special qualities for if you won't take him? He got the very best. If he only needs to be noble and unhappy, he could have remained more ordinary, don't you think?"

"Leave her be, Wjera, you'll see, she already has something new planned in secret, – maybe something much more beautiful," said a small blonde girl in an embroidered bib apron, "and if you don't leave her in peace, she won't tell us in the end."

"Do you have something? Do you have something? Is it beautiful?" they cried expectantly.

"It's nothing for you! But the most beautiful fairy tale of all!" the addressed by the house wall declared, "do you know the verses by Uhland?" And she began to recite with a soft voice:

"In love's arms, you rest intoxicated, Life's fruits beckon you; Only a glance has fallen on me, Yet I am richer than all of you.

The world's happiness I gladly forgo, And look up, a martyr, For above me, in golden distance, Heaven has opened itself to me."

They listened with very solemn faces until the last words faded in a kind of rapt adoration.

"Hoo!" said the pretty dark Wjera, really affected, and a second added, defeated: "Yes, then certainly –"

But the one who had recited just laughed. She laughed so from within, so freshly and with such convincing trills in her throat, that Erik up at his window almost started to laugh along, and suddenly felt in league with her. Some of the girls began to giggle. But most were put off.

"You have no seriousness about life!" said the first of the class reproachfully, and another even claimed: "She has no heart. She mocks her own thing and us with it."

Only the blonde, cute girl seemed to cuddle up affectionately to the laughing one and reminded her: "You promised to show us the 'Unhappy' one finally. Will you do it today on the way home?"

"Yes, I will. Because I want to leave him to you. Make him as happy as you want."

"So, you are thinking of another?"

The bell that rang for the start of class interrupted the chatter at this critical moment. Arm in arm, they strolled leisurely into the school building. But the narrow feet were still stretched out in the sun.

"Now I must see her," Erik thought and leaned forward with a serious face. The girls' conversation had quite struck him.

And he saw her.

Leaning casually against the gray-plastered house wall, her arms crossed high above her head, she sat on an upturned rain barrel, occasionally used as a bench in this popular fountain corner. She wore her decidedly ash-blonde, dull hair loose, so that it fell soft and curly over her chest and shoulders in some disarray. The deep red ribbon that should have held it together at the back of her head had slipped down and moved slightly in the breeze. It was the only colorful spot and ornament in the picture. For the entire slender figure was dressed in a loose gray-blue garment that bore no resemblance to the neatly made dresses, bodices, ribbons, and aprons of the others. Closed kittely over the narrow hips with a simple leather belt, it scarcely revealed the delicate beginning of the breast and gave the girl something peculiarly boyish. But above that rose an irregular little face that worked almost contagiously in its exuberant high spirits. As she sat there, her upper body bent back, her rather dark eyes lifted shining, her lips half open as if in beginning laughter or demanding thirst, so that under the too short and strongly curved upper lip, the white teeth showed – she made the impression of rearing up in overflowing zest for life, ready to break out joyfully at any moment, – almost involuntarily one thought of a thyrsus staff in the intertwined hands stretched up, – and the Bacchus boy was complete.

As she stood up quickly and suddenly and ran into the house, Erik rose from his leaned-forward position at the window and hastily gathered his notebooks. While he walked to his class, he laughed at his own astonishment. Two lambs in his flock certainly did not belong to the boring average: the holy Teresa, and then this wicked scamp and rascal.

Meanwhile, it had become lively in the hall corridor from all sides, in all corners, and for a few minutes it buzzed around like a swarm of gnats in the May sun. Then the noise abated, the classroom doors slammed shut; now and then a straggler rushed to his place; individual teachers, all in dark blue frocks, the prescribed uniform for these schools, passed each other greeting or stayed to exchange a few words in the corridor. In Erik's class, everyone was already mouse-quiet and in the best order when he entered with an animated expression. For a moment, he let his gaze wander over the blonde and brown girls' heads, almost all of which looked up at him with lively and attentive eyes. Although he stood on this spot and faced his young audience for only the second time, he already felt very clearly the mood of sympathy that shone from all these eyes. He owed it to his own openness. For they noticed very well the genuine interest he, as a teacher, brought to them – to the blondes and brunettes, the clever and the foolish, the willing and the rebellious. Whatever faults he might have had, he certainly didn't possess one: conducting his lessons like a lifeless duty machine.

Erik pushed the blue notebooks to the edge of the lectern and said, sitting down: "The notebooks can be distributed again. Most are of rather regrettable content. Hopefully, the continuation will be much better. Regarding one essay, however, I would like to inquire."

He opened the top notebook and read the name: "Who is Ruth Delorme?"

The called one seemed to have expected this question; she stood up before her name fell from his lips.

He gave her a startled look. It was the Bacchus boy from the schoolyard.

Now, she didn't make quite such a curious impression anymore. The neatly gathered hair and the "class seriousness" on her face disturbed him – perhaps also that she had lowered her eyes. He would have liked to run his hand over her face as if to remove a mask so that he could see the real Ruth underneath. But that would have been the mischievous, laughing boy from before – and that matched so little with the impression her essay had given him. The strange chatter of the girls at the fountain came to his mind.

"Impossible!" escaped him.

She looked up in surprise.

"But yes!" she said.

"She can! She can write verses!" some voices called out. You could hear the pride they took in this black art and how interesting they found the unexpected interlude.

"Verses, – that's possible," Erik replied, "they aren't even beautiful. Quite the opposite. But a schoolgirl –"

He broke off somewhat awkwardly and was annoyed. The remark was too stupid. They were all schoolgirls, and one of them had to be it. Had to? The thought occurred to him: perhaps it wasn't an independent essay?

He leafed back in the notebook. "There's an earlier essay here. Something literary-historical. That one falls way short in comparison. All laboriously traced lines – and false lines. There's a saying that in essays, external help isn't always disdained. Could that be the solution to the riddle?"

But while he spoke, he was already convinced that he was wrong and that she would proudly and indignantly claim that no one helped her.

Now she really shook her head and said: "No one helps me."

Again, he looked at her in surprise. How that sounded! Just like she had said under tears: "I am so utterly alone!" There was a quiet tone in it that moved him – something so completely new, unexpected, which he couldn't reconcile with the rest.

Suddenly, he could no longer stay on the lectern, in the calm posture of the teacher. A compelling feeling of interest found its expression in that he stepped down and approached her at the bench, in the midst of the others.

When he stood right in front of her, he became aware of a rashness and, if not returning to the place, at least to the role of the teacher.

"In the change of the title and the use of verses, there's a striking deviation from the prescribed; was there perhaps an exception made for you by my predecessor?" he asked.

"He preferred her! She was allowed to do what she wanted!" several shouted.

"She no longer belongs to the school! She only comes to some classes!" others called out.

"I'm leaving soon," said Ruth.

"Leaving? From the place?" he asked, and a burning regret overwhelmed him.

She lifted her eyes.

"No. Just from the classes."

As their gazes met, he saw her face light up. Not just her eyes, the light spread over her forehead and eyes like a smile, although she remained serious. The "class expression" fell from her features like a held-up veil.

He gave her a sign to sit down.

"That's very unfortunate," he then said, pacing up and down a few times, and it wasn't clear to him for whom it was actually unfortunate, whether for the teacher, or for the student, or for both. But he quickly added: "It's too early. The essay is not a sign of maturity."

Then, as he began the lesson, he did not address her again, avoiding calling her name during the hour, though he was preoccupied with the thought that she wanted to leave. But he understood that this lively interest in a remarkable child, even if it exclusively appealed to the educator in him, had to be fully mastered and clarified within himself before thinking of yielding to it in front of a few dozen curious girls' eyes. He was very familiar with the usual infatuations for the teacher, did not doubt that he was already the object of such infatuations, but tried to stick to not betraying himself by his behavior when a little student made an impression on him – which inevitably happened among people of flesh and blood.

Ruth sat still in her seat and followed his words and remarks with dreamy eyes. She was a rather distracted student, and so she now absorbed nothing of what he lectured, only noticing the manner in which he did so and his characteristic hand gestures. She noted that he had narrow, nervous hands of noble form, but they were slightly tanned, as if someone who had often exposed himself to air and sun, and this struck her as a contradiction that occupied her. The straight, somewhat stiff line of his shoulders imprinted itself on her like an image, and then that his hair, when speaking, fell in a tight little tuft into his forehead, and he always threw it back with a short jerk, keeping his head a little arrogantly raised. It was short-cut, smooth, thick hair, and it almost annoyed her that it refused to curl even a little bit, – just a little; in her thoughts, she let it grow long curls, but they looked funny, so she cut them off again. This made her laugh; she almost laughed out loud, and to be sure, she supported her mouth on her hands.

But with all this, she didn't look as if she were engaging in such externals in loose mischief, but as if she were straining, deeply immersed in thought, over a difficult problem. She had sat like this during his first lesson, unnoticed by him.

Ruth still made the same dreamy, thoughtful face when, after the end of the lesson, a whole swarm of girls gathered around her to go home. They had hardly been able to wait for this moment because now Ruth was supposed to show them the "Unhappy" one who dominated all their imaginations. Arm in arm, one behind the other, swinging their satchels, they walked laughing and chatting down the street and turned into the Nevsky Prospect, Ruth leading the way and not paying attention to them. Some looked around cautiously to see if anyone was following on the paths Ruth was leading them, but the street was fairly deserted, only a few maids following at a discreet distance, carrying the satchels for the most pampered, and behind these, Erik could be seen approaching.

"Actually, Ruth is a lucky one!" said the pretty Wjera to her neighbor, "that she can engage in such stories. I think her relatives don't care at all. Yes, it's quite different when you still have parents."

"Shame on you!" the girl next to her said indignantly and nudged her with the lunch box, "it's a terrible misfortune to lose your parents so early. Poor Ruth! Think, where she has been all her life – in Belgium and Germany, and always among almost strangers."

"Yes, that's how you get around," insisted the unfeeling adolescent, "even in a Swiss boarding school she's been. And I'd so love to go there."

"Even in a glass palace she's lived," one of them claimed somewhat uncertainly.

A burst of laughter erupted.

"Yes, in a dream! That's just a fairy tale she told. Listen, Ruth, she thinks it's real!"

"There he comes!" Ruth suddenly said.

The word fell like a shot into a flock of chattering sparrows. At first, they almost scattered, but then they gathered again, cleared their throats, adjusted their clothes, stretched their necks, and most of them blushed.

"Here, the blonde one?"

"No! The gentleman in the top hat."

It was neither of them. Ruth looked seriously straight ahead and into the face of a gentleman who was walking toward them. A young brunette man, in a light summer coat, with somewhat worn features, a small mustache, and almond-shaped eyes.

He seemed made for the hero of the tragedy – they all agreed on that. But while they were still staring at him like a sea wonder, the incredible happened before their eyes, which they hadn't actually believed in seriously: Ruth greeted him, she greeted him quite seriously, without changing her expression, but still as if an old acquaintance.

A half-smile crossed his face; he had fixed her firmly, now he reached hastily for his small round felt hat and greeted back. Quite familiarly, he did that.

The pretty Wjera almost screamed in surprise and delight, she had turned bright red, and to control her heart's movement, she involuntarily pinched her companion in the arm. A few of the others, however, kept a bit apart from the group, they were visibly embarrassed, walked awkwardly beside the sidewalk on the street embankment, and lowered their eyes. But the heroic stranger still found a considerable number among them who continued the game with eyes and expressions. As he walked past them very slowly, glances and smiles flew over to him, received clear answers, and were repeated. A couple of heads also turned back to look at him, and he, too, did not tire of looking back.

"No! That's too much!" one of the well-behaved ones on the street embankment broke out, "it's downright sinful!"

"Oh, dear virtue! It wasn't us who started it. Ruth did. She greeted him. And now she goes on indifferently as if it didn't concern her."

"Yes, what harm does it do?" several defended their behavior somewhat sheepishly.

"Certainly, it does harm – apart from being sinful," claimed the virtuous one, "have you never heard that one doesn't get married if one has had an affair?"

"Yes, she's right; it brings us into disrepute," a second one helped her, "and he certainly wouldn't marry you, don't imagine that. He can't marry you all!"

Some tried to mediate between the disputants.

"It's all nonsense. A mere fantasy story. So, let it be! Tomorrow during the breakfast break, we'll play with assigned roles again, then one of us will be the noble unfortunate, and all danger is over."

"No, now it's no mere fantasy story anymore. You shouldn't have shown him to us, Ruth."

She shrugged impatiently.

"I can't separate it like that. When we play it, we live it too. But do as you please," she said distractedly.

"No, first you have to think it further. Actually, it's very funny. Just like living twice: once at home and in school, – and then once more quite differently, where everything is just as you imagine it. – But we'd better not walk this way again."

"Oh, you cowards!" Wjera interjected, who had not participated in the argument until now because she was still dealing with the "Unhappy" who had remained standing somewhere at a street corner, "I find this story a thousand times more interesting than all the fantasies around it. What do we get from those? They only amuse us because we're kept locked up!"

Over their arguing, they didn't even notice that they had reached Ruth's home at Isaacs Square, meaning that most of them had moved quite a distance from their own homes. They followed habitually like a flock of sheep, but Ruth herself had gone straight home. Now she hesitated and fought between the desire to turn into a side street and the necessity to enter her relatives' house at the usual hour. There was still plenty of time until dinner, she wouldn't be scolded for a delay, and what she now had in mind was sweet and enticing like a spring fairy tale.

But there was something else that held her back: if she went in now, she would remain, as always, completely unnoticed and unobserved in the whole household; if she stayed out until late lunch, she might be noticed, questioned, bothered. And that decided it.

Like one of those little insects that adopt the color of the wood or leaves they sit on for protection against hostile forces, so Ruth, half unconsciously, behaved towards her surroundings. It was her way of defending herself.

Ruth broke away from the chatting group of girls and disappeared behind the high doors of a large stone building in front of which a soldier stood guard. A section of the War Ministry was located there, along with several large crown apartments, one of which Ruth's uncle, the state councilor, occupied.

Her disappearance signaled the general departure. Now some were shocked by the long delay and sought to reach a horse tram line by running or negotiated with the cab drivers who immediately gathered around them, loudly underbidding each other as much as possible.

They wouldn't miss Ruth until tomorrow, they had had an excellent time, had gotten quite heated! Tomorrow, when they were hungry for new nourishment, she would come again.

Erik had only followed the girls a short distance, as he had to teach at a boys' gymnasium and a private school. Then he went up to his city apartment, which was spacious and pleasant but located four flights up: in return, he could overlook the Neva River from the windows, where the Ladoga Lake still drove its last ice floes through the powerful blue waves. They shimmered transparently in the dazzling May sunshine. Erik rejoiced in this view anew every day.

After school, he usually stopped by here to take care of various tasks and pick up incoming letters, as the rural mail service was unreliable. Today, he had hardly entered when the doorbell rang.

He opened the door and stood there with a smile.

"Warwara Michailowna!" he said.

"What is this?" she asked, looking around quickly, "Already in the countryside? Moved? Alone here? I didn't know! Then you must have received my letter – –?"

"I found it here yesterday," he replied, leading her into the adjoining living room, where the upholstered furniture had already been dressed in their summer covers and stood around like ghosts in their white linen covers. The carpet had been removed from under the round sofa table, and a faint smell of camphor lingered in the air.

"I wanted to get your answer myself – or from your wife!" said Warwara Michailowna, sinking into one of the white-covered armchairs, "despite dust and sun, here I am. I need to know why you don't want to come."

She looked wonderfully pretty in the chosen simplicity of her spring attire, with her charming mouth and the melancholy in her deep dark eyes, which formed such a piquant contrast to her lively nature.

"Thank you!" Erik replied, looking at her, "but you are practically taking the answer right off my lips: I really didn't want to come. To bury myself in the countryside for a while. – Out there we can play such poetic games of tag and croquet when you've moved out too. – This winter, I've been too deeply immersed in social activities."

"And what harm is that? Just ask Klare-Bel if she doesn't also prefer to see you in a dress coat? The salon is your natural milieu. You are not at all like those German boors and philistines who sometimes come to us with their gold-rimmed glasses and blond full beards! Your family has only settled there for a few generations, – somewhere on the Frisian border, – French emigrants, – don't I know well?"

"You're going that far to prove that I should go to social events?"

She laughed and playfully tapped the ivory handle of her parasol against the table.

"You're a mocker. I only wanted to say: don't think that you were born to be a schoolmaster. Despite that blue uniform you're still wearing, – which, by the way, looks good on you because it's a frock coat. You were born to be a man of the world. If you avoid us – mondains – you're hurting yourself. – – I know it. Don't laugh."

"I'm not laughing. You're very perceptive, Warwara Michailowna. – Maybe too much so –?" She shook her head.

"You wouldn't please our spoiled society so much if you didn't get a little intoxicated by it yourself. Am I not right?"

"Well, let's assume I don't want to be intoxicated," said Erik, crossing his arms; "that you come as the tempter is indeed bad for me. A good thing the season is ending."

She pouted.

"I already know. You consider me the incarnation of worldly superficiality."

He did not contradict.

For a few moments, both were silent, and between them lay, impossible to ignore, Warwara's unspoken question: "Am I the one who intoxicates you?"

"You're an egotist," she said, looking up, "otherwise, you would have noticed that you're mistaken. Don't you know why I like to have you around, among people? Because I feel just as well as you do that this hustle and bustle is fundamentally vain and hollow, – devoid of content, – and it intoxicates me nevertheless, – like you. Your presence was thus that of a fellow sufferer for me. Hand on heart! Aren't we something like fellow sufferers? We share a common temptation."

He looked at her firmly. She spoke quickly, a little excitedly, with the soft, melodious tone he found so ingratiating in the Slavs. At this moment, she herself wasn't quite clear whether she was flirting with him or perhaps being more honest with him than ever with herself. It really seemed to her sometimes – and especially in the rare hours of solitude, – as if they were driven towards each other by a related urge. And then Erik was interesting to her: as a person. Like a hungry man among the satiated is interesting. Among the socialites of her circle, he appeared to her as someone impatiently searching for prey, and because he didn't find what suited him there, trying to dull his hunger with trifles.

"So: camaraderie in a shared temptation!" said Erik, looking away – "perhaps – a contest, who succumbs better to it?"

She stood up to leave.

"You may be right to mock, and it would only sound sentimental if I wanted to reply: no! More than that, – a shared longing," she replied, standing close to him, who had also risen, "you're a thousand times right. We've never spoken a serious word with each other. And a man doesn't need an ally. He can do it alone."

She spoke in all seriousness; it sounded almost genuine, and what she said matched so peculiarly with the melancholy in her dark eyes. For a minute, – a fleeting minute, Erik felt as if his imagination was deceiving him. A longing broke hotly within him, over which reason laughed, – and a wild, domineering desire to trample the laughing reason underfoot and make a beautiful self-deception come true.

Without knowing exactly what he was doing, he had stretched out his hand; it was an almost commanding movement, like a: "Stay!" He saw nothing clearly anymore; he only felt the nearness of this supple figure, these eyes from which longing emanated.

And suddenly, he kissed her with closed eyes on the neck and cheek. Not playfully, attempting. Quickly, vehemently, almost violently.

He muttered half incomprehensibly: "Make it true! Make it true! Don't let me wake up! Were you seeking me?"

At his unconscious kisses, Warwara was suddenly struck by fright. She had been intoxicated herself for a moment, but the force with which he responded sobered her just as quickly. Through his momentary excitement, she felt something of the deep, inner hunger and longing in him, which she had carelessly touched. She didn't perceive his kiss as an audacity that astonished or hurt but as a paralyzing danger to body and soul, threatening to engulf anything that came too close.

With a violent movement, she freed herself.

Her gaze ran over him. He should actually have seemed to her like a child, so full of life's demands and impatient expectations that it could no longer play. It breaks the offered toy violently to see what's behind it and stands there with a disappointed face.

She didn't want that. Rather play than be taken seriously – so seriously that her innermost being would be exposed and measured against impossible illusions. She feared the disappointed face.

Erik misunderstood the vehemence of her movement. But it also awakened him. He had only forgotten for a moment that she was playing. – His excitement dissipated immediately. Only some mockery remained in his eyes and around his mouth. Mockery of himself.

The air in the room was stiflingly hot. The sun seemed to shine almost unimpeded through the thin white window curtains, and the noise of carriages and horse trams from the street sounded discordantly.

Warwara had slowly walked into the anteroom, and Erik escorted her to the front door. They exchanged no words.

Only at the door did she turn to him and measure him with a peculiar look that he didn't understand. There was regret in it, but also rejection, a small superiority over him, the man, and then something like a slight admission: "I would like to be the one you need, and who could satisfy you, you wild one. But I am not."

"I assume: you won't come," she remarked distractedly.

"With your permission: no!" he replied, pondering her look.

The door closed.

•

Ruth appeared punctually at four o'clock, the scheduled lunchtime, in the dining room, which, high and large, furnished with dark mahogany furniture, lay in the middle of a series of rooms. She had brushed and groomed her outer self as smoothly as the uncle, aunt, and cousin used to, and sat silently in her place at the table, which a servant in white cotton gloves served noiselessly. During the meal, which engaged the participants extensively, the conversation remained quite monosyllabic. The uncle did not like long table conversations, and his wife was busy enough providing him with the right pieces.

Only when the green glass mouth rinsers, which no one used, were placed before each person, and the silver coffee machine, which the aunt always operated by hand, stood before her, did the conversation at the table become a little livelier. That seemed to be what Ruth had been waiting for. She quietly rose from her seat and wanted to leave.

"Are you going to your room already, my child?" asked the aunt, "then take a look at it. It shouldn't look so untidy and ungraceful in any young girl's room."

Ruth made a penitent face. "I will tidy it beautifully," she said hastily; "may I then go out again until tea time?"

"Until tea time? Is it something so urgent?"

"It is urgent," said Ruth. The uncle looked up.

"Who are you going to see? Is it someone from school?"

"Yes," Ruth explained, impatiently rubbing the door handle she was already holding.

"Tell the servant to accompany you and wait for you there."

The uncle watched her as she quietly closed the door behind her.

"She is a strangely convenient thing," he then remarked, lighting his cigarette, "I know no one who demands less and makes herself less noticeable than she does."

"Because she is granted everything," supplemented the aunt with her somewhat high voice, which made the Baltic accent stand out even more. She was a baroness from Livonia.

"Everything? Well, you know, another child wouldn't be so reserved. She knows, for example: this is the hour of the most intimate, undisturbed togetherness, – and she always leaves. But at nearly sixteen, one doesn't act out of tact."

"No, she doesn't do that either. You always idealize Ruth. She simply doesn't love us enough to attach herself more closely to us. Sometimes I think: maybe she is heartless."

"But Mathilde! how can you say something so bad about the little thing! Read the last letter from Belgium, how they praise her in the boarding school and want her back."

"Yes, one knows that, my dear. She was a profitable boarder. And then they are Catholic there. How can one trust them? I am the one who advocated for Ruth's move to us. After all, we are responsible for her. For her growing up in discipline and order. What good is it that her relatives there are of Flemish nobility? The views are the main thing. And one doesn't know those people there in that regard at all."

The uncle remained silent with a disgruntled face. He knew that for his wife, all people outside the small Baltic provinces were "those people," – while for him, it was just the opposite, the world only began beyond the Russian border. Not only did he find his wife's provincial exclusivity ridiculous, but even her Baltic homeland feeling. With his French name and the German and Slavic elements in his family, he felt so cosmopolitan that he never had an emotional relationship with any country or people. He didn't scold or complain about Russia, like most of his kind, because he considered it undignified.

"Ruth certainly wouldn't want to leave here now, Mama," remarked the daughter, "now that she's practically grown up. Nowhere can one be better introduced to society than here."

"But it seems to me she doesn't want that at all," replied the uncle with a smile, who loved accompanying his pretty daughter to social events, "she has already seen so much of the world and people and doesn't care about it. Thank God then, that we won't have the same circumstances with her as we've had with you for a year, Liuba."

"Now you really are capable of putting your own child down for Ruth," said his wife nervously, who had no ear for a joking tone, "let her travel to Belgium, for heaven's sake!"

"No!" he replied irritably, turned his chair away from the table, grabbed a newspaper, and buried himself in it. One of the most unpleasant qualities of his wife had always seemed to him to be her undeniable excellence, against which there was no appeal, but almost more unpleasant to him was her complete lack of humor.

The hour of the "most intimate, undisturbed togetherness" was thoroughly ruined.

•

Ruth, of course, had no idea that she was the innocent disturber of their peace from her empty place at the table; in fact, at the moment, she might have almost entirely forgotten which country on earth she was in, whether Belgium, Russia, Germany, or anywhere else. Her hands clasped behind her back, her head slightly bowed, she walked restlessly up and down her room, and her face bore the expression of intense thought, as it had on the school bench during class. Her cheeks were hot and brightly flushed, and from time to time she shook her head as if she couldn't quite come to terms with her thoughts.

After a while, she stopped, smoothed her hair from her forehead, and remembered her promise to "tidy up beautifully." That went extraordinarily quickly. Every single thing lying around was put into the nearest drawer, and when this was done conscientiously, it turned out that there were surprisingly few items left in the room that could have been arranged "gracefully" as per the aunt's instructions. It was a very cozy little room, with pretty furniture, a red velvet corner sofa, and even a knickknack shelf on which stood a glass pug. But it did not bear the mark of its owner, but that of a well-furnished hotel room. Neither crafts nor hobbies gave any hint about the nature of the person who slept, learned, and dreamed here. It seemed as if Ruth daily said to this environment, as she had earlier at school: "I'm leaving soon anyway."

When Ruth was finished, she hastily grabbed a soft English wool beret of light gray knit, put it on her head like a boy's cap, and called the servant from the servant's room next to the kitchen. He was sitting in his flowered chintz shirt, polishing knives, straddling a bench, and singing so that the knives flew in time. He was a young Tatar, very nimble and, as a Muslim, exemplary sober. Praying, singing, and sleeping were his favorite activities.

When he heard Ruth call, he quickly slipped into his dark livery and opened the front door for her.

She had him accompany her to the Finnish railway station; there she dismissed him.

"Now you can go to your acquaintances, Basil," she said to him, as he stood with his hat in hand at the carriage door, "but at nine o'clock you must be here to meet me again."

He nodded understandingly with his closely shaven head, which had a round, smooth-shaven spot on top, but looked at his little mistress somewhat worriedly. He wanted to go to "his acquaintances," but it seemed outrageous to him to let her travel out into the wide world so unprotected, especially in the evening, when there were so many drunkards on the streets.

"May I not ask for permission to accompany you?" he asked, struggling with the heroic decision to voluntarily forego his pleasure.

Ruth laughed at his crafty Tatar face, which just now looked almost trustful, and shook her head.

"Where I am going now, no one may come along!" she said solemnly.

During the ride, she looked out impatiently, like someone glad to leave everything behind; the short distance seemed long to her, as if she were really traveling far – far into a completely different world. But when she then got off at the small station building and had to ask for directions, she became anxious. What she had envisioned – compelling, irresistible, – was a very specific dream image, and as long as only her imagination painted around it, everything seemed to materialize by itself. But the reality, which now met her foreignly and interfered with the dream, intimidated her; it would have actually been nicer if everything had continued to form from within, as one lets oneself dream.

The anxious feeling did not subside but increased as she finally approached the house she was looking for. It felt as if she suddenly woke up and found herself all alone in a strange area. A formal fear overcame her out of sheer shyness, and she stood paralyzed at the garden gate.

There lay the house before her; a maid was sweeping straw from the broad gravel path in front, which was scattered all the way to the street, and beside her stood a boy with his hat pushed back, watching. He must surely notice her right away. She would have preferred to turn back.

"Close your eyes – run away!" she thought longingly. But she couldn't. She certainly couldn't abandon her own will.

A nightingale sang in the lilac bush at the fence.

And softly – softly, with a wooing sound, the second one called from the depths of the garden.

Ruth's eyes wandered past the house over the garden and remained enchanted by it.

"Spring!" she exclaimed joyfully, out loud. She had not yet seen it this year. Only now did she realize that she had just walked under green birches on the way from the station and that white anemones stood in the grass by the roadside. Now it seemed to her as if that had only been a little bit of spring that was scattered along the way by people coming out of this garden. But here spring was at home, from here it must come; and now she stood close to the gate, behind which it was blooming. In the red-golden scent that the sun wove around it, it looked like a fairy tale behind the old house with the newly blossoming fruit trees and the delicate foliage of the trees. Entering there was almost as if one didn't come out of a dream at all.

Jonas had curiously approached the garden gate where someone stood, whom he wasn't quite sure was a girl.

"I want to come in here!" Ruth said pleadingly.

•

Erik and Klare-Bel were sitting at the still uncleared lunch table in the living room by the terrace, and as always, Erik was telling his wife lively and communicatively about the small events of the day. Full of humor, he described the girls' school and Ruth. He only briefly mentioned Warwara's visit to the city apartment.

Then Jonas burst breathlessly into the room.

"Papa! Someone is here to see you. Her name is Ruth. I brought her to your study."

"But Jonas!" cried his mother, "how could you do that! It must still look awful in there! Bring her over, Erik! Please, bring her over! If only Gonne would clear away!"

Erik didn't hear anymore. He was already gone.

When he entered his room quickly, Ruth was standing in the middle of it, slightly leaning forward and pressing her hands firmly against her chest. The first impression he received was one of timidity, isolation, as in the moment when she had quietly said: "No one helps me!" Seeing her standing there, and she looking at him with large, anxious eyes, she no longer reminded him in the slightest of the boisterous boy in the schoolyard.

Erik only vaguely thought of the notion that one should offer a chair and say something kind in the case of an unexpected visit. All such etiquette seemed to belong to another world, – he forgot every conventional word in the presence of this shy, childish, visibly deeply moved figure. It was as if she were standing alone before him on a deserted island on the wide sea, – a child of the people –, and nothing around but a few hovering seagulls above their heads.

Quite instinctively, from this impression, he found only the word of joy: "You come to me?"

The "You" acted like a deliverance on her. It seemed to her in its simplicity a magic word that instantly transformed the foreign, heart-constricting reality, – transformed it into the dreamlike realization of what Ruth had longed for and devised.

She took a step towards Erik, a bright expression flew across her whole face, and pressing her hands more firmly against her chest, whose heartbeat took her breath away, she said childishly: "Thank you!"

He had seated himself on one of the standing chairs and took her hands in his. The hands trembled, and he noticed how pale and fragile she looked, if not for the expression of exuberant vitality that he had seen in her.

"Are you afraid?" he asked, and his gaze rested on her narrow face.

She nodded very slightly, and still, she trembled like a bird touched by a strange hand.

"You're not afraid of me, whom you come to? Tell me why you come."

She took off her cap and thought. She mentally went through the entire history of her decision, from the first impression at school, – but it was certainly too lengthy and confused to recount.

She tried to pick out the main point. But now she forgot everything. It was utterly impossible.

And suddenly Ruth burst into tears.

"My dear child!" he said gently, brushing her loose, curly hair from her forehead, which had fallen over her lowered face. Then he took her hands in his again.

"Do you trust me?" he asked.

"Yes!" she said softly.

"Unconditionally?"

"Yes!" she said again.

"Then you must neither tremble nor be afraid. Try very hard to control it. Very hard, do you hear? It will work."

She made an effort to suppress the nervous trembling that ran through her body. He waited quietly for a few moments until she succeeded. Then he persisted with his first question: "Now. And now tell me why you have come. Tell it as well as you can. Just try. I will help you."

She sighed and began uncertainly: "I will soon no longer attend school —"

"No. I know. And —?"

"And so I had to come here."

She paused to organize her thoughts, then added shyly, with a touching expression: "I am alone!"

Erik felt warmth to his innermost heart. Never before did he think he had felt such deep, holy tenderness as for this child. The desire to devote himself to her, to lay his hand on her as on something that belonged to him, suddenly became so strong in him that he instinctively took it as already fulfilled and accepted no obstacle.

"Would you like to belong here, Ruth?" he asked.

"Oh yes!" she exclaimed eagerly, then said fervently: "Always!"

Her face had changed, her eyes now looked very dark and laughed through the wet lashes. She would have liked to say again: "Thank you!" For it expressed all her thoughts and feelings in one word. But she hesitated to repeat it.

Erik looked seriously down, as if thoughtfully considering a plan.

"After leaving school, you would probably still receive various instruction," he remarked, bringing her back to reality, "at least that would be highly desirable. Would you like to receive it from me?"

She nodded eagerly.

"Good. We would then work together," – and in a light tone, he added: "a lot of work, Ruth! Will you be willing? In that essay there, – it led us to each other, didn't it? – well, there's almost as much to be alarmed about as to rejoice. I have never seen such a disordered little head with such tangled, wild, unfinished ideas and notions. Do you believe that?"

She only smiled and looked at him trustingly, as if she thought: "You will surely sort and untangle it!"

He looked at her silently, and again she seemed to him like a shy, tired little bird that had helplessly fluttered about and suddenly found itself in a soft nest.

Outside, the May sun lingered in the sky, and through the thin mist rising from the damp meadows beyond the garden, its rays fell almost red like liquid purple. The still curtainless windows opened directly onto the back garden.

A bitter fresh scent of birch buds wafted into the room with the mild evening breeze, and the passionate call of the nightingales sounded tirelessly.

While Erik looked at Ruth, a disturbing memory came to him.

"Tell me," he said unexpectedly, "who was that man you greeted on the street?"

She blushed slightly and became embarrassed, but there was a twitch of hidden mischief around her mouth. Two telltale dimples appeared on her cheeks.

"I – – – oh, him! I don't know him at all."

"But he looked at you as if you knew each other very well. How did that come about?"

"Yes, it happened like this," she began with a sigh and pondered, "– it's really not easy to tell. I chose him, but he knows nothing about it."

"Chose? But, dear child, no one can understand that," he said impatiently, "pull yourself together better, Ruth! Speak more clearly.–Well?"

"I will!" she said, intimidated, "it's just so hard! It was a mere story, – that we played among ourselves – in the schoolyard during the breakfast break, – and there had to be someone who looked roughly like that. And so – I chose this one, because it's nicer when you think of a real person."

"But what should he have thought of it? For example, just because you greeted him first?"

"I had to do that! How else would he know what to do? Whether he should greet?"

"And if he had started a conversation with you on the street? Didn't you think of that?"

She looked surprised.

"He wasn't allowed to do that. That wouldn't have fit his role. He had to be noble and unhappy."

Erik let out a short sound. His eyes looked serious, almost worried at her.

"In your childish game – yes. But in reality?" he asked slowly. "Can't you better discipline your thoughts? Can't you distinguish between them? You must, Ruth! And now tell me what you would have done if he had fallen out of the imagined role?"

She thought.

"Then I would have closed my eyes and run away."

"Would you have become invisible by closing your eyes?"

"I? No! but he would. Because then I would have had to find another."

"Another?!"

She nodded.

"There are many of them!" she assured him trustingly.

"And you would have really done that? Think carefully! Would it have still not become clear to you how childish and brazen your behavior was?"

Ruth looked unhappy. Apparently, he was reproaching her. She thought about what he could mean by that? She couldn't understand why she should care about the stranger outside his role?

"I needed him, so I took him!" she cried with a plaintive face.

Erik stood up and walked through the room a few times. Then he stood before Ruth, who had sat on the edge of his chair.

"Tell me, are there more such strangers you greet on the street?"

"Yes, all the streets are full of them."

"– Men?" he asked hesitantly.

"Also men. I always need fresh ones for school. Also women, children, old people."

"What do you mean by needing men 'for school'?"

"In the stories for the girls, there always has to be one. Preferably one with a little mustache. But I also have other stories, – much, much more beautiful, – wonderful ones," she added eagerly, – "and those with children are my favorites."

"Don't you tell those to the girls at school?"

She shook her head.

"They don't find them beautiful!" said Ruth sadly.

He sat down next to her on a leather chair by the window and leaned forward slightly.

"Will you tell them to me from now on?" he asked seriously, "but all of them, without exception. And without a corner where I can't look in. I must know and hear everything that goes through this fantastic, useless head. We will make a proper agreement: you won't tell anyone else. Only me. Always come here with everything. You wanted to belong here. – Will you do it unconditionally and obediently?"

Her eyes were large and filled with gratitude as they looked at him; he could see in her face how the thoughts in her struggled to find expression, but he still had no idea of the inner jubilation with which a new happiness dawned for her. She wanted to tell him so much, but in her word-poor feeling, she fell silent instead, and suddenly, as if she had to help herself with a gesture instead of words, she slipped from the chair and knelt beside Erik, – as if on a place now assigned to her, expectantly, with a look like a child at Christmas.

She felt so happy. At home. Safe. From here, everything good must come.

He gently stroked her hair. "So listen to the rest of our agreement," he said in a calm tone, under which she became completely still and listened, "if you give me your stories, then I will also give you something. You will not, as far as it depends on me, remain stuck in your own fantasy but learn to look far and wide with clear eyes, as far as life – the real, glorious life – reaches. And even if it requires effort from you at first, don't you think I will teach you something more beautiful than you have dreamed and imagined so far?"

"Oh yes!" she cried longingly, as if stretching both hands towards something awaited, – "that is it: of all the most beautiful fairy tale!"

He noticed the expression because she had already used it in the schoolyard with the girls.

"That's exactly what you said when you told the girls today that you had something new in mind. What was it?"

To his surprise, Ruth started and lowered her head.

Erik looked astonished.

"What was it?" he asked sternly.

"I can't say," she assured shyly, "please, please don't."

He grasped her hand firmly at the wrist so that it hurt.

"If it is something that is so difficult for you to speak out, then it is all the more necessary that you say it. I must know – now, Ruth."

She tried to pull her aching hand from his, and when she couldn't, she lowered her face even more, almost hiding it against his coat sleeve.

He bent her head back and looked into her face. It was flushed all over.

"It's no use hiding," he said unexpectedly gently, "you will always have to give in to me, my child. Make it short!"

Her hands clutched nervously on his knees, then she lifted them with a pleading gesture towards him.

"It was just – I got so tired of all these stories at once; everything stopped at once, – I didn't want to think of anything more. No matter how beautifully I thought it up, no matter how many people I thought in it, – I was always alone. The people greeted and walked by. And then – then such a longing came, – such longing for four days. I couldn't play anymore. Never more."

"Longing – where to?" he asked softly.

"Here!" she said in a quiet voice, turning her head away.

He let it free, let her hide it against his coat sleeve again.

He had both arms around her.

II.

Erik sat with Ruth's uncle and aunt in the drawing room, holding his hat and gloves on his knees and looking down at them thoughtfully while listening to the conversation.

"I think it fits well with your trip, Mathilde," the uncle said now, "because while you're in Wiesbaden with Liuba, Ruth will be completely unsupervised here. I really don't know what the little one should do with her long vacation since most acquaintances are going abroad this year instead of going to the countryside."

Erik had a keen eye for people's exteriors and was strongly influenced by them. He rather liked the uncle, with his ash-blonde hair, already a bit gray, and beard, his slight shoulders in his elegantly built frame, and his delicate, almost feminine hands. In tone and demeanor, he reminded Erik a bit of Ruth. In contrast, Erik felt a pronounced antipathy towards the aunt.

"Such visits to various acquaintances in the countryside wouldn't be a suitable occupation for Ruth now either," he remarked, looking up; "she needs something to do – real work and exertion. Even physical or mental overexertion would be better than a lack of occupation. At this age, one needs strong nourishment, and Ruth needs it most of all."

"You see, what do I always say?" the aunt interjected, nodding meaningfully to her husband; "I always say she is allowed too much freedom. But you always found that the most convenient."

"Dear God! What would you want to do with such a little woman," the uncle replied appeasingly, "you couldn't possibly have her scrub rooms?"

"No, you know, dear Louis! You really don't have to bring that up – it's as if I let Ruth do things only fit for the lowest servants!" his wife said, taking his playful exaggeration deadly seriously, "but overseeing a bit of the household – Ruth could certainly have done that. Liuba is also encouraged to do so. It is, after all, a woman's vocation."

Erik looked at the tall, imposing figure of the aunt with barely concealed mockery in his eyes, finding it characteristic of her entire being that the usual good forms of outward behavior couldn't quite conceal a certain lack of natural grace.

"As far as that's concerned," he interrupted impatiently, "you need not reproach yourself for that omission. In a household so well-served from all sides, the so-called 'household help,' whether it involves watering flowers or making coffee, is at best an indifferent game, – at worst, it creates the illusion of having accomplished something. On the other hand, I wouldn't object much to scrubbing rooms."

The uncle laughed heartily. "Now you've thoroughly spoiled things with my wife!" he teased jokingly, "but I must confess that I don't quite understand why both of you are so eager to put Ruth to work. Naturally, I have no objection to the education you suggested earlier, – on the contrary, I'm pleased for the little one. But I'd like to ask you not to carry out the scrubbing rooms even symbolically. Don't transfer it to the intellectual. Just don't make it too serious. Ruth is so used to running around and being happily lazy."

"I think you're mistaken," Erik replied firmly. "Ruth is neither lazy nor happy. She's used to exhausting herself entirely in a self-made dream existence. This has partly made her ahead of her age, but partly also left her behind her age. I've never seen such an uneven development. If she's not stopped in time, Ruth runs the risk of becoming mentally ill due to her imagination."

The uncle shook his head in surprise.

"That's curious," he said, "I've always thought Ruth was a very practical little woman. There's never been a trace of imagination in her. Everything she says is so direct and sober. And she prefers not to say anything at all. You should know how matter-of-fact she is in everything where young girls usually have their imagination! I've always liked that about her. Liuba can't compete with that."

His wife looked at him, hurt.

"Fortunately not!" she confirmed somewhat excitedly. "Liuba would never walk around dressed like in a gray sack just because it's more comfortable. And besides – imagine, the other day I hear my daughter say to Ruth: 'just wait, when you're a year older, then you'll know what's beautiful and ugly, and you'll ask the mirror: how do I look to him?' – – My God, you know how young girls talk among themselves! But what does Ruth answer to that? She just laughs and then asks in astonishment: 'Why not rather: how does he look to me?'"

At that moment, the door opened, and Ruth entered.

She came from her room, unaware that there was a visitor. When she unexpectedly saw Erik, she recoiled and turned bright red.

His sudden presence among her relatives, who were so distant from her, – the unwanted mingling of an image that filled her completely with the surroundings she avoided and fled, made a very strange impression on her. It was as if a dream figure from glorious fantasies descended into real life to have a banal conversation; – as if the most intimate, which didn't even have words, was translated into the language of the common people.

That Erik had come here, that he even had to deal with her relatives, didn't occur to her in the slightest. He should have arranged it so that it remained an affair from another world – from her world. Otherwise, she would have rather run secretly to him at night on bare feet.

She looked terribly red and awkward, pressing herself, embarrassed and with a shy face, into the door gap. But she didn't feel embarrassment, rather an inextricable mix of anger and shame, – shame that something delicate, belonging to her, was shown and discussed before foreign eyes.

"Well, Ruth, is that how you behave?" the aunt reproved, "can't you come closer?"

Then she did something strange. She raised both hands in front of her eyes and, thus with a blinkered face, walked like a child afraid of strange guests, through the room to the carved round sofa table around which they sat.

The uncle laughed, his wife shook her head disapprovingly and said reprimandingly: "Such a big girl!"

Erik, who had turned his head to her when Ruth entered, looked at her silently and attentively. When she stood right next to him, he raised his hand and pulled hers away from her face. "Why don't you want to look at me today, Ruth?" he asked.

She didn't answer. She was still very red and kept her eyes down. This "you" that he used to address her, and which had so gratefully moved her yesterday, almost hurt her today. It sounded completely different – here, in this place, – it sounded like the address one chooses for a child standing among adults. Yes, she stood opposite him and the others, and they were discussing her as if she were betrayed and sold, – as if it were not her – her own, very own affair.

Through Erik, she felt betrayed and sold.

"You're seeing Ruth from a charming side," the uncle said, still smiling, "but she's not as bad as she looks. What's gotten into you, little one? I've never seen you embarrassed before."

Erik, who had been looking at her intently, now tried to divert attention from her.

"We'll get along," he said warmly and turned to the uncle with a question about the time and day of the planned lessons.

Ruth stood indifferently beside them, not paying attention to the exchanges between the others. Only the redness gradually left her face, making way for an expression of repressed sadness and disappointment. She didn't look up but studied the shiny pattern of the parquet floor intently.

Then, just as Erik was about to take his leave, she heard her uncle say: "If it's really not too much of a sacrifice for you, we'll expect you here in the afternoons after your school hours!"

"No!" Ruth suddenly interjected loudly. It was as if she woke up. Her eyes flashed from one to the other in astonishment. "Here? That's a mistake. I'll come out there."

Everyone looked at her in surprise as she stated this so categorically, without a trace of embarrassment. Erik, however, rose quickly.

"That might actually be better," he agreed with her involuntarily, "and if Ruth doesn't mind the way and then spends the evening with us, it would indeed be preferable during these summer days."

He no longer spoke with quite the same confident superiority as before but somewhat hastily. A faint reflection of what had so distressingly and disturbingly touched Ruth about the situation now seemed to transfer to him as well, as if he suddenly sensed or understood her angry shyness. When he saw her eyes directed at him so reproachfully and with an unchildlike, almost stern look, it suddenly seemed strange to him that he had wanted her anywhere other than in his own quiet room, – where she had come to him. The chance had almost arranged it so. But she allowed no chance. Clearly and compellingly, like a vision, stood before her eyes what she had longed for and dreamed of.

While Erik left the room with her uncle and the aunt went out, Ruth remained standing motionless, her hands on her back, her head bowed, as always when something occupied her deeply. In the hallway, she heard the front door close, then a quick step on the stone stairs. Then it became completely silent.

She saw the room as if through a veil, bathed in dazzling sunlight that shimmered through the tall potted plants and palm clusters in both window corners and flashed on the gilded frames of the paintings, which had already received a thin tulle cover against dust and light.

Ruth walked slowly to the chair where Erik had previously sat. She sat down, placed both arms on the table, and rested her head on them.

And then she began to cry bitterly.

**

At lunch, the uncle observed Ruth thoughtfully. He had been so impressed that Erik seemed to understand everything going on inside her. There she sat now, so silent. Of course, you couldn't know what she was thinking. But that teacher couldn't either. He wasn't a mind reader.

"What are you thinking about all day?" Uncle Louis suddenly asked irritably.

"Me? About nothing!" she assured him with a surprised look.

"But you must be thinking about something. Every person does. What were you thinking about just now, for example?"

"Just now I was thinking about Grandpa," said Ruth.

This pleased the uncle, and he looked at her kindly. He had loved his father infinitely.

"You were only five years old when your parents died, and you came here, do you still remember him?"

She nodded, and the first fully conscious and clear memory from her childhood appeared before her eyes: a general's uniform, a snow-white large mustache, and above it two kind blue eyes – almost childlike eyes.

"Once he lifted me out of bed, – he looked so beautiful, with ribbons and stars, – and he was all glittering, – and then his burning cigarette touched my bare arm. I cried a lot. And then tears came to his eyes, – but real, big tears, so that his eyes were full of them. And then he hugged me and kissed me – on the arm and the bare neck and face and all over. – That's how Grandpa was. – Now I would gladly let my arm get burned if only he would kiss me like that once more!" she added wildly.

You could see it boiling inside her. She had never been able to forget Grandpa's affection.

"Do you have pictures and keepsakes of him?" asked the uncle, thinking about what he could give her.

She shook her head.

"No pictures. Just a cracker. He once brought it to me from the Emperor. From a gala dinner. I was so sure there must be golden clothes inside. But Grandpa said there were only clothes made of thin tissue paper with a small edge of tinsel. So I didn't let the cracker pop. I still have it. – And so there are still golden clothes inside."

The uncle smiled. Erik no longer impressed him as much. Grandpa's kisses, crackers, golden clothes, and clothes made of tissue paper, – those were certainly normal and harmless fantasies of a child's mind.

**

When Ruth left for her first lesson the next afternoon, Uncle Louis gently pulled her earlobe and whispered: "If you should run away from him, I'll protect you!"

**

But when Ruth stood at the garden fence of the country house this time, the thought of running away didn't occur to her. Nor did she hesitate so long to enter, but pushed open the gate and walked straight ahead, – not up the back terrace and into the house, but further into the depths of the garden, which had so enticed her the first time.

There stood Jonas among the fruit trees, busily searching for caterpillars among the small leaves. There weren't any caterpillars yet, really. But he couldn't wait to pick them off.

When he saw Ruth coming, he took off his wide-brimmed straw hat and looked embarrassed because he had thrown off his jacket due to the warmth of the sun.

"Papa is in the house!" he remarked eagerly and bent down to pick up his jacket lying on the grass.

"Yes! He was standing at the window," confirmed Ruth, leaning against the thick trunk of an old elm. He had nothing to say in response, so they both remained silent for a few moments.

"How beautiful!" said Ruth then, entirely immersed in her spring, and raised both arms towards the mighty, gently swaying branches above her.

Jonas looked up intently but saw nothing.

"Where is the beauty?" he asked, puzzled.

"These funny little elm leaves! The other trees already have much larger leaves. But these are still so tightly packed in the buds, – and all together at the tips of the branches, – as if they didn't dare. Or as if they were looking at the sticky brown husks they've already thrown off. Doesn't it look like little bouquets scattered on the tree? It looks as if they just flew up there. And as if they could fly away again."

"They don't fly away," assured Jonas and turned back to his supposed caterpillars.

"No. Only these do," said Ruth and stretched her hand towards the cherry tree from which, under Jonas' careless touch, the delicate petals floated down onto her arm.

"These are good cherries. Hopefully, the translucent red ones, because those are my favorite to eat. Otherwise, we mostly have apple trees and ordinary pear trees," Jonas remarked.

"They look just as beautiful," replied Ruth; "when you stand at the fence, it looks like a fairy tale. But later they become as green and natural as the other trees. Just smaller."

"That's how it has to be," explained Jonas indifferently, "otherwise, the lawn would never get proper shade. And that's the best part of summer. Because right here by the fountain under the fruit trees, my mother lies in the deck chair. And she can't stand too much sun."

Ruth looked at him with interest. It seemed special to her that he rejoiced over the trees and the shade for his sick mother's sake and found the green leaves better than all the beautiful white blossoms. The schoolgirls she knew mostly had mothers too, but they tended to be healthy, and she had never heard them say they looked forward to summer for their mother's sake, but always only for the vacation. And they were girls. But this was a boy.

She looked at Jonas more closely, and he pleased her very much. And he also looked over at her every moment, and she pleased him greatly.

"Is she very sick?" she asked timidly after a while.

"Not very. She just can't get up, – hasn't been able to for many years," he informed her; "when she wants to, Papa takes her in his arms and carries her. He does that wonderfully. Sometimes she also has pain and cries. And then Papa always has to be with her, and that helps her."

Ruth involuntarily turned her head towards the house, where the sick woman lay and where he was, who carried her and helped her when she was in pain.

"Behind that window," said Jonas and pointed over the terrace to the living room; "her chair has just been brought inside because of the sun."

But in the broad frame of the open window was only Erik's figure, his back turned to them. And now he slowly turned around.

Ruth hastily pulled away from the trunk she was leaning against. "Now I'll go in," she said.

After seeing Ruth enter the garden from the street, Erik had indeed gone to the living room window and occasionally looked over to the fruit tree group where she stood and chatted with Jonas.

Klare-Bel lay next to the window, occupied with a laborious and intricate piece of needlework, consisting of retracing the pattern on a damaged damask napkin. This work was called "Mazen" in Holland. And those who took it seriously wanted the "Mazen" to extend to mending stockings and underjackets.

"Is Ruth still not coming in?" she asked after a long pause.

He checked his watch.

"No. It's still a few minutes until the time," he noted briefly.

"That's really no reason not to come in if she's already here. But maybe she much prefers standing in the garden and chatting with Jonas than sitting in the room and learning, Erik. That's also quite natural in the end."

He remained silent and looked down at her needlework with an expression of impatience. He couldn't stand the "Mazen" and claimed it ruined the eyes and even the character.

"Please stop stitching for a moment," he said, simply taking the needle from her hand, "I don't know, – this stuff makes you nervous."

Then he looked at his watch again.

He had a premonition that it wouldn't be as easy to gain determining power over Ruth as he had thought on that wondrous May evening. She didn't want to be disturbed in her independent dream life by any unexpected or undesired movement on his part, and even if she raised him to the hero of her "most beautiful fairy tale," he had to remain completely still and comply with all her intentions, – otherwise, she would quietly slip away from him again, as quietly and dreamily as she had come into his life.

That couldn't be; the educator in him couldn't allow his plans with Ruth to fail. He knew he wouldn't rest until he had her will completely in his hand. But what a gentle hand he wanted to have for her then!

Besides these pedagogical considerations, an impatient joy filled him. Joy over the struggle that lay ahead with Ruth. Erik, who understood others far better than himself, had no idea how much a youthful, domineering desire stirred under the guise of the pedagogue.

He turned to the garden.

"Now she's coming!" he said, and indeed, it sounded like a sigh of relief.

His wife suppressed a smile and resumed her work. "Well, good luck, Erik! Just don't forget we're having tea at nine. I imagine you'll make her hungry and thirsty."

He had gone over to his study and was already opening the door from the inside when Ruth arrived and was about to knock.

"Finally!" he remarked as she entered, "do you know, Ruth, what my wife just suggested? She thought you would certainly prefer being in the garden with Jonas than here in the room with me. What do you say to that?"

She looked at him uncertainly and sat down at his gesture in the leather armchair by the window. Then she replied with downcast eyes: "I came because I wanted to, – only because I wanted to. That Jonas is also here, I didn't know at all. That's just a coincidence. I found him here."

He didn't immediately understand what surprised him about her answer, which wasn't really an answer. She exclusively emphasized that she was here entirely of her own free will. She cautiously avoided a comparison.

"If it doesn't turn out the other way around in the future, my dear child," he said, arranging some booklets and books on his desk, "because chatting with Jonas or walking around in the garden you will only do in the future if you 'want,' that is, if you happen to be in the mood for it. Here, however, where you've come of your own accord, it can't quite stay that way. Here, something definite must necessarily await you, something independent of the moment and its moods. So, something you might sometimes think: 'I don't quite want it like that, – I didn't mean it quite like that, – this should be different, – that should not be there today.' Isn't that so?"

She remained stubbornly silent, making a closed-off face. Indeed, what he said had crossed her mind. But the fact that he could know this was very unpleasant to her.

He stood by her and took off the wool cap she had kept on.

"Well, Ruth, yesterday you didn't want to look at me, and today you don't want to speak to me. Is this how you keep our agreement? And I had hoped you would tell me a lot. A lot – everything. All your most beautiful stories."

"No," declared Ruth, "never. I don't want to tell anything. I want to keep everything to myself."

"You miser!" he said, laughing, "that's very bad. Isn't it bad to invite a guest and then slam the door in his face? But fortunately, you can't do that anymore, Ruth. Didn't you give me your stories? Did you forget? Now they're my property. I can do with them what I want. I can take them out of your head and keep them all to myself."

"Oh no!" she said a little more lively and involuntarily reached for her head, "that's impossible. It doesn't work if I don't want it."

"You talk a lot about your will, Ruth. And that you're only here because you want to. But do you really know why you want it?"

She paused and looked up. When she didn't find an immediate answer, he added: "I know it for you: you wanted to have this will clarified and trained by someone who cares enough about you. All learning is only a means to that end."

Ruth placed her hands on the armrests of the chair, and her face became even more rejecting. "As if she had put on a visor!" thought Erik, looking at her. But behind this visor, increasing agitation worked in her. The passive mood in which she had come today did not stand up to Erik's pressure, but even less could she recapture the dream and the strange happiness of the first evening. So, she instinctively closed and hid from him, like before a power that must be closely examined before engaging with it.

"Everything is different today!" she muttered.

"It will always be different from what you arbitrarily imagine," he replied calmly, "and it should be, Ruth! It should be too serious for a mere fantasy game. You see, I too have devised and dreamed something beautiful that I would like to see realized in you. I promised you: for the stories you wanted to tell me, you would experience one through me. The Most Beautiful, – didn't you say so? With telling, you can do as you please, but with experiencing, you will do as I please. It was my gift to you. And even if you don't want to know about it today, you will have to accept it."

Ruth became uneasy. She knew only two kinds of people, and the fact that she couldn't place Erik in either of them frightened her. One kind consisted of her daily surroundings, which were mostly disturbing or indifferent to her and slid off her ineffectively; the other consisted of strangers she observed from a distance, taking the external stimuli for her fantasies from them. Erik couldn't belong to these, because they only did what she wanted, – they were only what she wanted. He, on the other hand, was a reality that invaded her. But she couldn't fend him off as she fended off her own; there was something there that attracted and stimulated her more powerfully than all the shadowy images together.

She looked at him timidly.

"I'd rather come another time," she asked quietly, "I can't learn today. I can't."

"Yes, you can," he replied soothingly, "and deep down you want to. But we can't start the fight over this every time. It must be decided once and for all. You or me, Ruth! One of us must obey."

Then Ruth suddenly jumped up and said indistinctly: "Then I can also stay away."

It had escaped her quite spontaneously, against all deliberation. But now it was out.

Erik saw that she stood pale and shocked at herself, and a strong pity for her seized him. It seemed to him that he had mistreated her, and his gaze softened greatly.

But he didn't think of giving in to this soft feeling. He wanted to bring the decisive situation to a sharp resolution. He had no doubt about success. And full of joy, he felt: once it was over, he could throw all strictness into the attic. Then he was Ruth's for all – all time, secure.

"Of course, you can stay away," he confirmed calmly, "if it really wasn't about more to you than such a pastime as you have in the schoolyard among yourselves. Do you remember what you said about the stranger you drew into your childish game? 'If he didn't suit me, if he fell out of the role I assigned him, then I would simply have to find another, – I would close my eyes and run away.' Is it the same or even similar here – – then run away."

While he spoke, he constantly felt great pity. She looked up only once, and as she encountered his soft gaze, it was as if her passive resistance turned into a kind of attack, – as if she were looking for a weapon, for something that could free her from her suffering, hurt him, and give her power. He recalled the words she had used about the stranger: "I just needed him, so I took him!"

Ruth grabbed her wool cap lying on the desk and squeezed it aimlessly in her hands.

"I want to go home!" she repeated and trembled all over.

"As you wish."

"So, goodbye," she said and walked slowly, as if paralyzed, towards the door.

"Goodbye, my child."

She had trouble finding and pressing down the door handle; her hands were cold and wouldn't obey her. But as the door opened and she stepped into the hallway, she looked back into the room with burning eyes as she closed the door.

Erik sat on the leather chair by the window she had left. He had propped his right arm on the armrest and covered his eyes with his hand.

And suddenly Ruth was overtaken by the awareness that all his desire to rule was, in essence, just a desire to serve. Suddenly it overcame her: that he was suffering right now, – suffering because of her, who had hurt him.

It hit her with a feeling of pain, but this feeling was strange and intoxicating: it contained triumph. It was a pain that felt like happiness.

She still trembled all over, but no longer with the fear of fleeing. In the midst of the fear of her flight, she had stopped, turned against the enemy, and seen him defeated.

Whoever saw Ruth walking through the hallway might have thought she was intoxicated.

**

At nine o'clock, – Gonne had already brought tea and toasted bread slices to the table, – Erik finally came into the living room.

"Nothing has happened, has it?" his wife asked, glancing at his face. "Ruth left so early. And I thought she was supposed to stay with us?"

"For today, it was better this way," he replied, and Klare-Bel didn't ask further.

But Jonas did.

"I like Ruth very much," he assured, "is she coming back soon, Papa?" "Soon!" he said.

"Just think, she didn't want to tell me," Jonas continued chatting, "I spoke to her in the garden when she was leaving. She looked so strange, Papa, her eyes were so big and shining, – she looked as if she had just received a gift."

"A gift?" repeated Erik and put the teacup he was about to lift to his mouth firmly down on the table.

"Yes, absolutely, that's exactly how she looked. But she didn't answer me, and then, at the gate, she asked me for a glass of water."

"She didn't feel sick, did she?" asked Klare-Bel, concerned.

"No, but she was trembling. I fetched the water for her from the well. And then she left. – But I watched her for a long time," Jonas added.

"Surely you were too strict with her, Erik," said Klare-Bel, "I could already tell when you went over."

"Too strict? But, Bel, then you don't look as if you've received a gift."

He spoke in a light tone, but what Jonas had told him occupied him. It was something new, unexpected, which he couldn't immediately make sense of. He understood her defiance and even that she ran away, he understood well and accounted for it. But this here, he didn't understand. Was it possible that she left gladly – with joy? – – And that she wouldn't return?

**

While they were still having tea, a heavy thunderstorm gathered outside. Klare-Bel looked anxiously at the window, through which you could see the dark, black-yellow bank of clouds in the sky. A storm wind swept through the treetops, shaking and bending them; the daylight, which the long May evening had still spread over the garden, disappeared abruptly. And soon after, under glaring flashes of lightning and mighty claps of thunder, a heavy downpour beat down.

"Please, close the windows! Please, Jonas, stop eating! Oh Erik, the thunder!" said Klare-Bel, closing her eyes at every flash.

Erik stood up, paused for a moment at the window, and looked out into the turmoil, then closed it and returned to his wife. The fear of thunderstorms was something that had overtaken her since she had to lie helpless. As a young woman, she hadn't known such fear, and Erik wouldn't have tolerated it in her. Now he was patient with it.

"If only we could light a lamp! It has become so dark all of a sudden. And then the lightning is so terribly bright, Erik!"

"Gonne doesn't need to bring a lamp in," he replied with a smile and placed his hand over her eyes; "aren't you safe now, Bel?"

She nodded gratefully and pressed her face against his hands.

It was a severe thunderstorm. Lightning and thunder followed each other incessantly. For moments, the garden looked as if illuminated by Bengal lights, and in the bluish light, you could see the leaves and blossoms torn loose by the storm flying wildly in the air.

Whenever the thunder cracked particularly loudly, Klare-Bel jumped.

"I wonder if Ruth was home before it started?" she asked.

"Long ago. She must have been home before we sat down to eat," he reassured her, "and the servant will be pleased that he doesn't have to fetch her in this storm."

It lasted quite a while before the lightning and storm even subsided a little and the coarse-grained rain drummed more softly on the roof.

"Well, Bel, now it's getting better," said Erik and took his hand from her face. He reopened the window, through which the cooled evening air now flowed in fresh and fragrant.

Jonas stood at the window on the rain-sprayed terrace, leaning over the railing, looking into the devastated garden. A large elm branch had fallen across the gravel path, the fruit blossoms had paid for the natural upheaval with their lives.

"Now they have indeed flown away, all at once, the white blossoms," Jonas called regretfully, "just as Ruth said! How sorry she will be. She found them so beautiful. But up there, it's already turning blue again, Papa."

"Thank God!" said Klare-Bel. "Such excitement and confusion outside are terrible. You get drawn into it."

"Yes, it's nothing for you anymore, my poor one," said Erik, "but there were times when you had to endure such thunderstorm tempests and the roar of the sea, without me being with you."

"That was also dreadful, Erik, quite dreadful," she assured, shuddering, "back then when you went out with people when a ship was in danger. And that one time, you know when you were the only one who persuaded Niels and the others. Because they also had wives and children. But you've always been so good at persuading people: 'It will work!' you said to them, and they believed you."

"You believed me too, Bel, when you had to stay behind alone, and when it seemed to you as if it wouldn't work."

"Yes, Erik. Sometimes I thought the fright would kill me. But then you said so confidently: 'When I come home, wet and tired, Bel, I have to find my wife there and the little boy, both happy and healthy.' Well, and then it had to be so."

He was silent. Before his eyes stood a stormy night, where he, returning from real danger to life, had found his wife, with the child next to her, kneeling in the middle of the small room and praying loudly.

For a moment, he had almost been bewildered, standing on the threshold because he had never seen her pray. When they married, a few devotional books had come into his hands among her belongings, and when she saw him leafing through them, she asked him:

"Do you believe in what's written there?" He had looked up with serious eyes and answered: "No, Bel." Since then, this subject had only been touched upon once more in conversation after years, and then it had dawned on him with inner amazement that his wife, without even really noticing it herself, no longer had her faith. When he asked her how that had happened, she had responded with her friendly calmness, surprised: "Well, Erik, if it's not true, what use is it to believe in it?"

And when he now entered that stormy night in his high seaman's boots and his wet wool jacket, she stopped praying and stretched out both arms to him with a cry of joy. He lifted her from her knees and kissed her. "Do you do this, Bel, when I'm not with you?" he asked her softly.

"When you're not with me, Erik!" she said, crying, "because then it always seems to me that I have to!"

At that time, she was pregnant with their second child. Shortly afterward, she had the dangerous fall that cost her health, and the child was born dead.

When Gonne came in with a burning lamp, Erik was jolted out of his thoughts.

"I'd like to go over to my study now," he remarked and kissed his wife on the forehead, "I still have schoolwork for tomorrow. As soon as you're tired, you must have me called."

In Erik's room, it was already almost dark. Only a few rosy clouds that had broken away from the large cloud mass and now swam cheerfully around independently on a wide piece of blue sky, cast a faint glow through the windows. In this light, you could see the desk, the bookshelf, and the old leather sofa against the long wall fairly clearly.

Erik stopped and stood on the threshold.

For a moment, he clearly thought he saw Ruth sitting on the leather chair by the window. He couldn't be hallucinating.

With a feeling of annoyance at himself, he resolutely closed the door behind him and grabbed a candlestick from a side table to light.

Then he started and put the candlestick down again. There really was someone sitting on the chair. "It's me!" said a plaintive voice. "Ruth!" he called loudly.

It was her. Soaked to the skin, in clothes from which water dripped heavily onto the floor and hung torn on one side. Her teeth chattered audibly.

Erik had her in his arms and touched her worriedly and tenderly with caressing hands, – her chest, arms, and the tangled hair that clung so tightly and wetly to her cold little face.

"When – when, – where did you come from? Weren't you at home?"

"I wasn't at home," she said timidly, nestling frostily against him; "I came back from the city station. And ran here. Just as it started. I don't want to go home," she added pleadingly, "I'm so cold!"

"My darling, you shall not go home! You shall stay here! But how long must you have been sitting here already? How could you do that? And nobody heard you ring the bell at the terrace door?"

"I didn't ring. I was ashamed. I climbed in through the window. But it was hard," she admitted, and mouth and eyes smiled impishly at him.

"And then? What if I hadn't come in here anymore?"

"Then I would have had to sit here all night!" she said, shuddering, and rubbed her head against his arm like a wet cat. And then she said very quietly: "Because I couldn't say it to the others. And yet I had to say it. That's why I came back! I had to say: I will do everything I'm supposed to."

A quarter of an hour later, Jonas was on his way to the station to send a telegram to Ruth's uncle saying she had to spend the night out there. Ruth herself was well wrapped up in Jonas' bed, which Gonne had hastily prepared for her. Then she drank hot tea and fell into a restless sleep.

Jonas felt very proud when he heard on his return that he had given Ruth the most important piece of furniture a person possesses, his bed. And full of enthusiasm, he stretched out that evening in Erik's study on the old leather couch, whose padding left nothing to be desired in terms of hardness and inexplicable bumps. Jonas was too excited to fall asleep quickly, and every moment he peeked through the door crack, asking what Ruth was doing now.

She had a high fever and spoke wildly and incoherently in half-sleep.

"The sandcake," Erik heard her say anxiously several times, "it's pressing on me. It has become bigger and bigger. I'm afraid. It's swallowing me. And at first, it was so soft and small and so wonderful to knead!"

Erik kept watch over her until morning.

She tossed and turned restlessly in the pillows and kept talking to herself in broken sentences. But it seemed to him that these weren't actual fever fantasies but contained a clear coherence. He had the thought that she might often talk to herself this way without anyone hearing, and that now the fever had perhaps only given the violent impetus to do so unconsciously in front of human ears.

He could gather from her words that she was still occupied with the storm walk. Sometimes she mentioned it in a way that she hadn't made it herself at all, but as if she had been pushed against her will along the way, – driven out into the storm, lightning, and thunderclaps by force. She saw herself walking along the lonely, dark path while hail and wind blew against her, and her feet stuck in the deep, soaked clay soil.

And this was then mixed with another fever image: the attempt to run away from something without being able to, as happens in dreams.

"I run and run, and don't move an inch!" she complained restlessly, and the fever increased when she thought about it.

The next morning, Ruth was fever-free. When Erik, fully dressed for school, entered her room, she sat up in bed, wearing a nightshirt of Klare-Bel's that was too short and too wide for her, and looked at him with shy eyes.

On the bedspread lay scattered flowers that Jonas had sent in very early. Even a few almost intact branches from his cherry tree were there. He had torn them off with total disregard.

"Do I have to go home now?" Ruth asked anxiously.

"No, my darling. You shall stay here and not just lie here sick but also jump around healthy. My study is still waiting for you. Weren't we going to work together?"

»Yes!« she said eagerly and made an effort as if to stand up, causing the flowers to slide off the blanket.

»But, my dear child, not right now. Later!«

»Later!« she repeated obediently, leaning back and closing her eyes.

Erik took hold of her wrist and checked her pulse.

»When I come home from the city today,« he remarked meanwhile, »I will find you in the garden, in the sunshine, and completely healthy. Right?«

»Yes,« she said obediently, without opening her eyes. But there was an expression of suffering or sorrow on her face that worried him.

He bent down to her and gently brushed the hair from her forehead.

»But not just healthy, Ruth,« he added, »but also happy! Not this withdrawn, closed-off expression! You mustn't close yourself off from me again like this, my child. Do you no longer like being with me? Does it not feel good to belong here?«

She opened her eyes and looked at him fully.

»It feels as if I had fallen into the sea,« she said.

•

Erik left earlier than usual to visit Ruth's relatives before his school hours began. He found them at their first breakfast. Basil reluctantly let him into the dining room upon his explicit request, where the aunt, still in her morning cap, was behind the samovar. She seemed a little puzzled by the overly early visit. The uncle, already about to go down to the ministry as he did every morning, sat in military trousers and an elegant closed jacket, having his last glass of tea. He jumped up and approached Erik with lively, concerned questions about Ruth. Erik explained that she had turned back on her way home, gotten caught in the storm, and fallen ill from the excitement.

»The poor little thing!« the uncle said in a tenderly concerned tone; he quietly reproached himself for having actually encouraged Ruth to "run away." »How terrible it must have been for her! Just going unexpectedly from warmth to cold makes Ruth's skin shudder all over, and she trembles. And then she can get so terribly frightened.«

Liuba came in, greeted Erik, and poured herself some tea with sleep-reddened eyes; she had been out in company and stayed up late.

»Yes, Ruth has no courage,« she confirmed, »when we once put a caterpillar on her neck, she fell into convulsions.«

Erik looked at her with a shocked expression.

»Did she show any tendency towards that?« he asked slowly.

»No, never otherwise!« the uncle replied irritably, »that was years ago. She must have been about thirteen. It was somewhere in Switzerland. Ruth was wearing a thin summer dress with a bare neck. It was very mean of you to scare her like that, Liuba. You should be quiet about it.«

»We didn't mean any harm,« said Liuba, »why did she always sit so absorbed and deep in thought, like a stone that neither sees nor hears. It disturbed the others' play. And since nothing would wake her up, we put a privet caterpillar on her collar. But the caterpillar crawled into the neckline. Ruth didn't even scream. She just collapsed.«

»You've forgotten the most important part,« remarked the aunt, »what excuses the naughty girls and explains Ruth's fright. As a child, Ruth was firmly convinced that the devil himself was in caterpillars, snakes, and all creepy-crawlies. She was always full of godless nursery tales. God knows where she picked them up. In such things, Ruth has always been strangely childish and still is. She still has the same horror today.«

»But everything that could remind her of it has been removed from her sight since then,« the uncle said to Erik.

»That shouldn't have been done,« Erik replied firmly, but his face had become very thoughtful. »One cannot be too careful with Ruth, but at the same time, one must handle her firmly if one wants to help her.«

He stood up to say goodbye.

The uncle was silent for a moment, crushed the end of his cigarette on the ashtray, and then suddenly said warmly to Erik: »You know, – I'm glad, really glad that Ruth is with you.«

»I want nothing more than for her to stay with me!« Erik replied simply.

»Yes, you see,« the uncle continued, stepping close to him, »I believe that with you, the little one has finally come to the right place. After all her wanderings. And the right place, that means almost as much as: home.«

»But please,« the aunt interjected, unpleasantly touched, »from your words, anyone would think Ruth was mistreated here.«

»Oh, how so mistreated,« he said crossly, »no, treated well, of course, how could it be otherwise? But why should we deny it: You know how to care for her better than we do. I felt it already the other day, today I know it clearly. I enjoy her too, – yes, I do, God knows, – but otherwise: the child gains nothing from it. That is just what I mean.«

»Well,« the aunt conceded, »we certainly have to be grateful to you. But don't speak so sinfully. It almost sounds as if you wanted to get rid of Ruth. Give my regards to the dear child. And if she should get sick, I will definitely come out and take care of her.«

Erik promised to give his regards to the "dear child" that he would have preferred never to return. He left with the uncle and considered a plan for which he hoped to gain his support. They had become close friends.

•

When Ruth got up late in the morning, she saw Klare-Bel's long chair already set up by the stone fountain. A piece of striped canvas, stretched between the fruit trees, protected her from the morning sun.

After the storm, the foliage around seemed to have unfolded as if by magic. The garden stood lushly green, and the last leaves were pushing out of their buds. Ruth walked slowly through the garden, her eyes delighting in the fresh, sun-warmed beauty around her and the sick woman resting in the midst of it.

»Good morning, Ruth!« Klare-Bel called out to her, stretching out her hand affectionately, »welcome, my dear child! You know who I am? I couldn't come to you when you were sick last night. I am glad you are well again and that you can now come to me.«

Ruth took the small, soft hand that showed how round and rosy it had once been, with dimples over the knuckles. Following a sudden impulse, she bent down and kissed the hand. She looked at Klare-Bel with a kind of reverence, as if she were the most precious thing in the house.

»Erik and Jonas are in the city,« Klare-Bel said, »I am lying here all alone. Will you keep me company for a while, Ruth?«

Ruth nodded, still without speaking; she was as if intoxicated by the spring and the strong, fresh scent everything around her exuded. She would have liked to shout with joy.

»I will stay here,« she declared and crouched with her knees up on the mossy stone edge of the fountain, from whose cracked water urn above her a long, thin vine dangled down like a snake; »because here it is the most beautiful place in the whole world!«

»She exaggerates everything!« thought Klare-Bel, secretly observing her, but she felt pleasantly moved at this moment. »It is even more beautiful at the sea now, Ruth,« she said, »where we used to live, – on the small island far out. Have you ever been to the sea?«

»Yes, several times,« replied Ruth, »but I would have much preferred to be right where you lived, – on the small island. But I didn't know about it back then. No, I didn't know.«

It seemed visibly wonderful and actually incomprehensible to her that she had ever known nothing about it. Klare-Bel found that she spoke quite like a child: something so self-evident with such a serious and moved face.

»And you know everything about it!« Ruth added with the same expression, »everything, just as it was. Was it beautiful?«

Klare-Bel was not a talkative person; she spoke as little as Erik spoke much. But she felt a great desire to talk to Ruth.

»Shall I tell you about it?« she asked, smiling at her.

»Yes!« said Ruth urgently, and a feeling stronger than mere curiosity entered her gaze, »but everything! how the people were, and the life, and the house, and the sea, and also the school children.«

Klare-Bel thought one should start with the house. And after describing how village-like small, and yet wonderfully cozy it had been despite its low-beamed ceiling and narrow window panes, always fogged by the salty air, – she moved on to the people who came and went there. Many people, – a whole crowd it seemed to Ruth, – and Klare-Bel's story always gathered them around the one she placed at the center, the one who shared everything with them and did everything with them, and whom the youngest child and the oldest woman greeted with the same smile.

Ruth's eyes sparkled. What Klare-Bel told, she believed she could perceive, see, and experience; she unconsciously completed the picture to the most tangible clarity by painting it with the golden colors that Klare-Bel herself mixed on the palette. And around this whole picture, she constantly heard the mighty sea roaring and foaming.

She smelled the salty air and felt the fine sea sand crunch under her feet; her imagination followed the hints of the woman, who didn't realize how lovingly she idealized what she described to Ruth, with poetic speed.

When Klare-Bel finished, Ruth breathed deeply, her cheeks vividly flushed.

»Oh, how wonderfully you tell,« she exclaimed gratefully, »I would like to do nothing but listen to you all day. All day. Oh, how I would love to experience that! How beautiful it must have been!«

»It was indeed,« confirmed Klare-Bel contentedly, to whom it had never seemed as beautiful as today during her own telling. She hadn't spoken of herself at all yet, only of Erik. But in response to Ruth's exclamation, she added with the pride of a woman who has lovingly earned her happiness: »Beautiful and also hard, Ruth. For it is hard to have to share so much with so many, all of whom want advice, help, and participation from the same one, always claiming and always taking him away. It is not easy, one must become modest. That you would have to learn first.«

»That?« said Ruth, perplexed, »no, I'd rather not. I hadn't chosen that. But to stand among the people and do everything as if one were a wizard, – that must be wonderful. It must feel like suddenly being many people at once – and then even more than all of them together.«

Klare-Bel was struck by these words. She felt the enthusiastic admiration in Ruth's tone, but she couldn't understand how this enthusiasm, far from wanting to serve the admired one, simply selfishly wished to take his place.

Ruth meanwhile lost herself completely in the picture she had painted for herself. After a short pause, she began again: »And that was just a village. A quite ordinary island. Surrounded by water, so that everything ended there. But it could have been something much bigger, right? Maybe with many more people on it. I don't quite know how. But I think: to be so strong, – and then to be allowed to do something mighty. It doesn't have to stop at the village.«

Klare-Bel found these words curious. She thought to herself, perhaps that was somewhat like what her husband had once wished and hoped for. Back when everything around them was still future and hope.

»In the end, it might not have stayed with the village,« she said, looking at Ruth, »only circumstances prevented it. He had such great plans before. Oh, what plans he had! But then came the misfortune that I had to lie down. And the doctors came, the trips, the operations. Lastly, the debts. That was the end of the plans. All that cost terribly much money, Ruth. And all for nothing.«

Ruth looked with wide-open eyes at the woman who could say that so calmly.

»I couldn't survive it!« she exclaimed involuntarily, horrified.

»Oh, my dear child! You think that when you are as young as you are. But then you learn to submit to fate and its will. Even to the hardest: lying still and no longer being able to provide for the well-being of those you love with your own hands. For that is the hardest, Ruth.«

It sounded so gentle and loving, how she said that in response to Ruth's thoughtless word. Not a single complaint for herself. She only regretted not being able to serve the others anymore.

But Ruth thought it almost indifferent whether one could still serve others in such a case. What horrified her so much was the idea of becoming the cause of a strong, healthy person stopping to serve his purpose because of such a misfortune.

It confused her entirely that she didn't pity the gentle, sick woman at all. She had the feeling: she would pity her if she only had the time to think about her. But she had to think about Erik all the time. And she felt pity for him, stormy pity to the point of tears.

Klare-Bel lay straight, looking up at the clear blue sky with her calm blue eyes. She thought of the happiness she might have retained, – so clear and blue and calm again.

»I wish for you,« she said to Ruth, who had fallen completely silent, »to one day be able to serve someone you love from the bottom of your heart. To be healthy, beautiful, and good and clever on top of that! No matter whether he achieves great or small things in the world, – that's not the point! The loving and the serving are more beautiful. Especially for us women. It is much more beautiful than being the one it's for. We don't need to envy that.«

»Oh no!« Ruth exclaimed fervently, »it can't be possible that it is more beautiful. The one it's for has it better. Otherwise, God would be worse off than humans!«

Klare-Bel threw a startled, reproachful glance at her from her blue eyes. But she didn't know what to reply. One really had to have quite a bit of patience with Ruth. Klare-Bel only felt secure as long as Ruth listened. She listened so nicely. But as soon as she spoke, one had to be amazed and actually also annoyed. She was certainly more suited for Erik than for herself. He would probably figure her out. For that was his specialty.

Meanwhile, Jonas had come into the garden from the street side, cheerfully whistling, and disappeared into the house among the trees with his school bag on his back. When he reappeared, the bag was off, and in his hand, he held a big buttered bread, which he bit into.

He ran over to his mother, kissed her, extended his hand to Ruth, and said: »You – you – have – « he stopped and blushed.

»You!« Ruth decided earnestly and looked at him.

»Yes, right?« he said cheerfully and sat next to her on the edge of the fountain, »because now we are housemates. Actually siblings. Right, Mama? And peers too. How old are you?«

»Seventeen in eleven months,« Ruth said.

»I'm only sixteen,« he confessed sheepishly, but then his face cleared up, – »that is now. But in eleven months, not anymore. Even sooner. Now you should eat a piece of buttered bread with me, because it's still a good hour until we have lunch,« he added and broke his bread in half in his eagerness to share it with her.

»I don't want to eat,« said Ruth, laughing at his eagerness.

»Then you must still be sick!« he claimed. »But that was also a real stroke of luck, you know, otherwise, you wouldn't have stayed with us at all. It was a good idea of yours to walk around in the storm. Just think! when you could have sat comfortably with Papa.«

»Yes. If I had stayed, I would have left too,« Ruth remarked pensively.

Jonas couldn't quite understand this case, so he quickly said: »Come with me to the grove, Ruth. You haven't seen it yet. There are so many nests. And a little stream flows through the middle, down to the meadow. We can easily climb over, the fence is very low.«

»No,« she replied, »you go to the grove. I have to stay here now.«

»What do you want to do here?«

»I have to think.«

»Think?«

Jonas looked at her somewhat puzzled; however, it seemed to be an occupation that demanded respect. So, he sighed and went into the house, as he didn't know how he could join in.

Ruth didn't notice him leaving. She remained seated with her knees pulled up, her arms on her knees, and her round chin resting on her clenched hands like on two columns. She stared intently at a single spot in the grass where a white daisy stood, and thought deeply, like an Indian fakir. She knew exactly where she had left off when Jonas came and made her stop.

Klare-Bel lay quietly with her eyes closed. The midday sun shone warmly over the trees, and not a breeze stirred the fragrant leaves. A couple of yellow butterflies fluttered around the spring beds, and at Ruth's feet, the crickets chirped their song loudly and eagerly.

Ruth sank deeper and deeper into her midday sun dream. As if in golden light waves, it wove around the figure that Klare-Bel's stories had conjured up before her. An unclear longing, half humility, half demand, took hold of her to see this figure as radiant and shadowless as possible, – in a warm glow that set it apart from all other beings. Why? Ruth didn't know.

But she did know: in this light, the real people she knew seemed even more disturbing and senseless than before, – almost as if they were mere bodies with hardly anything inside. And the fantastical shadow figures she imagined after real and foreign people, as beautifully as she wanted, and wiped away when she wanted, – looked much more shadowy than before, actually thin, and so transparent that one might think they were merely will-o'-the-wisps of thoughts.

Ruth wandered through the whole world like the Creator on the sixth day, but found only chaos again. And in the middle of it, the only person who, if he wanted to, could animate everything, whom imagination and reality combined to form. It was as if he stood alone before her in this lonely, fantastic world of her dreams, – the first person on the sixth day of creation, unrecognized yet, and a wonder. She stood still before him in astonishment, as if she had to ask: »Who are you? How did you get here? How dare you rule here?« He occupied her thoughts so strongly, he amazed her so much, that she lost herself in her thoughts and just looked at him. It seemed necessary to her that he be something special, remarkable, completely incomparable if she were to tolerate him there.

And again, the restless desire rose in her to heap brilliance upon brilliance, light upon light, on him.

After sitting silently for a long time, Ruth straightened from her crouched position and walked slowly to the garden gate. With her arms crossed over the fence, she looked down the road Erik had to come along. He came soon.

His first glance fell on her face and remained attentively and searchingly fixed on it. She looked quite pale and thin after the feverish night, but the suffering expression from the morning had completely disappeared from her childish features. A new expression, open and longing, which Erik liked, lay in her eyes.

He nodded at her with a smile. They didn't speak to each other, only Ruth's hand slipped quietly into his. Hand in hand, Klare-Bel saw them coming towards her.

»How long did you have to wait for me in the harsh sun today, my poor dear!« he said to his wife, »now you shall not lie here a moment longer.«

With that, he moved her chair closer to the terrace, lifted her out, and held her small figure as gently as one cradles a child to the breast.

»You too light burden!« he joked and looked cheerful and lively.

Klare-Bel laughed with delight and had her arms around his neck.

Ruth grabbed a slipped pillow and followed them up the steps. She would have liked to carry the whole chair and everything with it to do exactly what Erik did. The pity she had felt for him during Klare-Bel's stories had not vanished, – and in its place remained admiration. It now seemed completely natural to her that the sick woman didn't feel like a burden and hindrance on the healthy man's path, but that she laughed and clasped her hands around his neck.

When Ruth took her place at the table, she completely forgot that it was the first time she did so and that she had wanted to run away the evening before. She felt like a long-time housemate, – content and effortlessly fitting in with the others.

»I brought something for you from your uncle,« Erik said, seating her next to him at the table, »namely the permission to stay here as long as you want. I think we should answer him: all summer. What do you think?«

She nodded only and looked happy. If he hadn't been constantly paying attention to her and serving her himself, she would have preferred not to eat a bite.

When they were having coffee and the children ran outside, Erik looked at his wife and asked: »And now, Bel, how do you like her?«

»Oh, Erik! I like her well for you. Because she has something so incomprehensible, I find. That is just for you. Something to puzzle out.«

»She's a shy bird,« he said with a smile, »and it's not yet certain if I've caught her. One wrong move, – and she'll fly away from me.«

»Yes, Erik, I think that would make me extremely anxious. It would make me dizzy. Like a confusing embroidery pattern.«

»Uncertain? No, Bel, on the contrary. One becomes aware again of what one is capable of, – whether one is capable. One gathers strength, – the forgotten, rusted strength. And so one finally returns to the great security of life and the old belief in oneself.«

»Yes, yes, Erik. If only everything goes well.«

He stood up and warmly put his arm around her shoulders: »Worrywart! Just this once: let go of the worries, the gray ones! I am happy! You will see: on that girl I will grow my masterpiece!«

She sighed and silently agreed with him. That he took Ruth in was roughly like a scholar somewhere unearthing a really undecipherable manuscript, – she thought; he would rather and more eagerly read that than the best-written book. It was just the way it was: his talent and his calling lay there.

Erik left, he wanted to go to the train station to have Ruth's luggage brought over by a farmer's cart; her uncle had already sent it out.

Klare-Bel lay and thought. She forced herself to think about the time she always pushed back in her memory. It was nice that Erik could be so happy again and so full of sanguine hopes. That was better and more natural for him than those long, long years of suffering when he was filled with only one thought: how to make his wife well again.

A single years-long struggle, – a painful, horrible one.

Klare-Bel had to endure nameless things for the sake of his tenacity of hope, which never waned, left nothing untried, still ran up against the impossible, and with tireless defiance always resumed the old battle. It was not easy because Klare-Bel could not be anesthetized due to a slight heart weakness. But he always managed to persuade her to new ventures, new tortures, and with his boundless influence, to compel her. He became a doctor in this fight; what he had previously pursued out of passion and natural talent became his profession. He threw all his undivided strength into it: he didn't want to believe, didn't want to allow that a single stupid and blind accident could ruin happiness for life.

And now, since he had to believe and allow it, it was still hard to have sacrificed everything for nothing that his hopes had also hung on. And if Ruth could give him just one of them back, Klare-Bel would love her. It was no more than a small, late, and inconspicuous flower for a whole bouquet that life had owed him.

Never had this become as clear to Klare-Bel as today, since the conversation with Ruth by the fountain in the garden.

Jonas came in and sat at the foot of her lounge chair. He picked up a bundle of yarn that Klare-Bel had begun to unwind and held it on his fingers for her.

»Will Ruth stay with us now, Mama?« he asked.

»Yes. You heard it. Aren't you happy about it?«

»More than anything. Only now, I'll strive all in vain.«

»What do you mean by that, my child?«

»I mean: Papa will certainly prefer Ruth over me. Absolutely. She is clever, – don't you think?«

»I can't possibly know. But what nonsense, Jonas. Because Papa loves you, he wants you to try harder and progress better.«

»Oh, Mama, I already try as hard as I can. I also make progress. But Papa is so hard to satisfy. He is the strictest teacher we have. They all fear him. But I most of all. He demands the most from me.«

»You should be glad about that. – Just don't get jealous now, Jonas, do you hear?«

Then he laughed all over his face, seemingly without motivation, so that he really looked simple.

»No, Mama, I certainly won't. At least not in the way you mean. But if it should occur to Ruth, – to prefer Papa over me – –«

»But Jonas –!!«

He let the yarn slip from his fingers, almost tangling it.

»Sorry, Mama. I'll fix it right away. – You know, you were right when you said I should be glad Papa demands so much. That's exactly what Ruth finds more pleasant than it is. She'll realize that. And I will never demand anything unpleasant from her.«

»You're really a very silly and useless boy!« Klare-Bel said angrily and looked at her offspring more closely. He made a completely innocent face. The laughter had hidden in the corners of his eyes. »If Papa heard something like that! And then you wonder if Papa might prefer Ruth to you.«

»I don't wonder at all, Mama. I could never blame him for it. How could he not like Ruth better than me?«

»Where is Ruth actually?«

»She ran up to the attic room where Gonne is still tidying up. To set up her place, she says.«

When Erik returned from the station and Ruth's head looked out of the open window upstairs, he went up to her. The small, sloping room was already in order. Besides the bed procured today and a large wooden chest, which had almost the appearance of a real washstand thanks to neatly crinkled and pleated muslin curtains, there wasn't much to see yet. A smell of soap and freshly applied oil paint was noticeable.

Ruth sat on the narrow windowsill, to the sides of which small white curtains were already hanging; the ladder still leaned beside it. A light breeze moved the branches of the old elm tree in front of the terrace up and down, almost touching Ruth's face. From up here, one could only see the tree tops, and Ruth thought it looked funny: like a green, rustling wave, which one could imagine floating in the air, without trunk and root. How many birds must nest in it during summer! And under the overhanging roof, right above the window, clung two nests from the previous year.

When Erik stepped onto the threshold and noticed the arrangement of the room, he began to laugh.

»It's truly a real detention room, made for naughty children who have to serve a punishment,« he said and stood in the door frame, »or for runaways who must be locked up by force. Don't you think so, Ruth?«

»No. It's very beautiful!« she replied emphatically and almost took offense that he could make fun of her room; »it's just not finished yet, and that's the best part. When I'm in it, it will finish itself. It's very beautiful. Just the way I want it.«

»That's indeed the main thing, my little queen,« he admitted with a smile and came to the window. »When we first traveled back from abroad, our rooms in our city apartment didn't look much better either. And I liked it quite well too. One could start fresh and according to one's own liking.«

She turned halfway to him and looked at him with interest.

»Oh yes!« she said, »but besides that, it must have been terribly hard, – leaving the small island and coming here, away from the sea and all those people?«

He had placed his hands on her frail shoulders and gently pressed her backward, as it secretly worried him that she liked to lean forward so much.

»Why hard?« he asked calmly, »there are enough boys and girls here to teach, – naughty little girls with very naughty essays, as you know.«

»Oh those!« she said with deep contempt and shrugged, »they're not worth it.«

»Not even you?« he asked doubtfully and looked at her attentively from the side.

»No, not even me,« she replied honestly.

»You're incredibly humble today,« he remarked, »too humble, Ruth. That's not good.«

»Why is that not good again?« she asked distractedly.

»Because it doesn't come from within you, girl. Not from your nature. It's like trying to hold a position that makes you contort. You shouldn't do that.«

She didn't reply, perhaps hardly listening. Her thoughts were directed at something else she didn't know how to bring up. After a small pause, she said softly: »You look so happy. In your eyes – and altogether. Why?«

»Because I have you again, my child,« he replied seriously.

»Me! but all the others?«

»Whom, Ruth?«

She couldn't hold it any longer.

»I mean: just teaching boys and girls who aren't worth it, and nothing else! Instead of being allowed to do something completely different, something much, much greater, – as big as a sea with all its ships on it,« she tried to explain, fiddling with his watch chain without realizing it.

He looked down at her in astonishment.

»Are you fantasizing, child? You mustn't give in to that,« he said urgently, »what have you been imagining? You must be able to say it clearly. Well?«

»It's something real!« she exclaimed timidly, »it's no fantasy. We talked about it in the garden – this morning.«

»With my wife?«

Ruth nodded.

»She told me. About before and now. She tells so beautifully! She tells so wonderfully.«

»Does she? But what did she tell you?« he asked, and his gaze was searching and tense.

»Everything. And then, – yes, then it seemed so terrible to me, – so impossible that nothing came of it,« she said passionately, and her fingers clutched the watch chain as if she had to break something, »nothing but a schoolroom. And that it should always stay that way. It can't stay that way.«

She spoke almost angrily, and large tears stood in her eyes.

Erik didn't respond immediately. His hand lifted and gently stroked her loose, soft hair, and when Ruth wanted to look up, his hand slid down and covered her questioning eyes. He looked over her, into the green, rustling treetops, and fought down an emotion. He felt strange. He knew that what Ruth felt did not come from his wife; neither the passionate perception nor the fantastic vagueness of the regret was possible for his wife.

Never, since he had been married, had he spoken to anyone, had anyone spoken to him, about the disappointments of his life. And there she stood, who had known him for four days, in anger and grief and tears, and mourned these disappointments as if they were her own.

As several minutes passed in silence, Ruth bent her head lower, and her hand slipped from his watch chain.

»I promise I'll never say it again!« she said softly, apologetically.

He grasped her hand tightly and pressed it in his own.

»You must always tell me everything, everything that occupies you,« he replied quietly, but his voice sounded changed and subdued, »never hide thoughts that upset you from me, – and now, of all times, worries, my child, – such childish and fantastic worries.«

Then he leaned against the windowsill, his face turned away from the light, in the shadow.

»I want to tell you a story, Ruth; shall I?«

She nodded obediently, without raising her bowed head; one could see that she didn't care much about this story, and that she felt treated like a child.

»Once there was a man,« he began, »who greatly desired to cultivate a large, vast field, – a field as big as the sea. Because he knew the soil was good, and there were very few workers, – far too few. But it turned out differently than he had wished, and he was not allowed to work on the great field. Only at the very far end was he assigned a small piece of land where he could plant cabbages and potatoes. Just enough to live.«

She had long since raised her eyes to him with understanding. Big, impatient, they clung to his lips. Her entire soul was in these eyes.

»And then –?« she asked breathlessly.

»And then,« he continued, »one day he found a strange little plant among his cabbages and potato plants. Somehow its seed must have fallen into this soil. It was only a small, delicate sprout, and one couldn't yet see what was in it. But maybe it could grow into a little tree. And if that succeeded, – if a good gardener continuously worked on this little tree, and if the little tree allowed itself to be treated and bent, grafted, and pruned, – then – yes, then it could eventually bear rarer fruits than anything else that grew on the field.«

»Am I the little tree?« she asked naively and quietly slipped off the windowsill.

He didn't answer but drew her closer to him, so her hair touched his shoulder. Her face had an expression that wasn't a smile nor seriousness, and yet like an enhanced reflection of both, resembling ecstasy. It suddenly reminded Erik of that essay titled: »Bliss!« For the first time, this narrow child's face with its eloquent eyes and curved lips reminded him of the verses in the schoolbook.

»Would you like to be such a little tree for the gardener, Ruth?« he asked her in a half-whisper.

She took a deep breath.

»I'd rather be the gardener,« she said unexpectedly, »but maybe it's almost the same.«

III.

Every morning, very early, before the house was awake, Erik and Ruth would meet in the study. They both got up a couple of hours earlier than usual to do this, and every morning he would go over her work for the day with her, which he then left her to do on her own.

It was always the same scene: Ruth was always already there, leaning against the open window, waiting for him. She listened to the little chaffinches outside and at the same time for his footsteps coming down the hall. She usually looked a bit pale and anxious because, as carefree and happy as she could be with Erik during the day, she feared him as a teacher. And even now, when she heard his footsteps in the hall, her heart would start to race, and the old shyness would overcome her, just like on the very first evening.

It was always the same: without her turning around, Erik would come up close behind her until her back was against him, then he would clasp her hands in his, so she was trapped between his arms. For her, it was not just a caress but also something soothing and compelling at the same time, under which she instinctively held still and collected herself. And then, without any loss of time or transitional conversation, he would take her seriously and soberly in hand. Thus, the morning greeting would imperceptibly turn into the morning work.

One morning, when Erik opened the door to his study, he stood still for a moment, surprised. The white-painted shutters inside the windows had been closed so that the gray rain-light outside could only seep through the cracks; a single light burned dimly on the desk. Ruth sat there, surrounded by notebooks and books, writing without looking up.

Erik said nothing. He pushed back a shutter and opened the window so that air and light streamed in broadly, then he came to the desk and blew out the light, while Ruth looked up, startled.

He bent down to her, took her face in his hands, and looked at her attentively.

»You've been crying. About what?«

She blushed and hesitated for a moment.

»I don't want to be stupid!« she cried out, beside herself, with sparkling eyes.

He laughed.

»You're not stupid. Did I say that? At least not hopelessly. As long as I don't give up on you, you needn't give up on yourself.«

He pushed her chair back from the desk and took the pen from her hand.

»But you must not get up at night to work. Never without my knowledge. That's nonsense. When I've reviewed your work in the evening, then you're to stop.«

»The sun didn't stop either,« said Ruth, »it shone brightly almost all night. In the woods, a cuckoo was calling, and the thrushes under my window were talking. So, I came here quietly.«

Erik reached over her shoulder for the notebook she had been writing in, but Ruth held onto it hesitantly and shyly. It was clear that she was almost suffering in her agitation.

»Calm down!« he said earnestly and removed her hand from the notebook.

He read in it silently for a while, while Ruth sat with a furrowed brow, her hands clasped behind her neck and quite pale.

Then he placed her work in front of her.

»You did well,« he remarked, »did it cost you effort and self-control?«

»Yes,« she admitted honestly, without changing her posture, »but it doesn't matter.«

»No. It doesn't matter. Do you see that now? It was of no use to indulge you in what you liked and found easy; through what is hardest for your little imaginative head, through what is most difficult for it, that's where it has to go.«

He unclasped her hands from behind her neck and held them in his.

»I know it's sometimes been a hard compulsion,« he said, »and you've had to suppress your own nature; it hurt, didn't it? But it had to be. And now – now I'm gradually getting you just the way I want you, girl. Isn't it nice?«

»It's wonderful!« she exclaimed, turning back to him with shining eyes, »that's what I always think when it's hard for me! I try to forget and just think how wonderful it must be to get someone who is completely different to be just the way you want them!«

A shadow of disappointment passed through Erik's eyes.

»Is that all you think about, Ruth? And I thought it should make you happy.«

»It does!« she explained, surprised, and stood up.

»What do you want to do this morning? Let's go to the garden. It's not raining anymore. Or do you think you could sleep?«

She shook her head, laughing.

»I don't want you to be left alone later, without occupation and morning freshness,« said Erik, »you shouldn't work. Maybe you should come to school with me. The girls are still waiting for your promised visit. And in a few days, school will be out. It will distract and amuse you. And if it tires you out, all the better.«

Gonne had set the breakfast table on the terrace, and Klare-Bel was already lying in her chair next to it when Erik, Ruth, and Jonas came from the garden only after repeated calls. Jonas looked completely heated, his straw hat hanging on his neck; in his right hand, he carried a tall bucket, which he had obtained from Gonne and now set down on the steps leading to the terrace. A steel-colored, bluish-glossy snake, about two feet long, coiled inside.

»Oh, Jonas!« cried Klare-Bel, horrified, »how can you bring such a horrible creature here! Can't it bite us all to death, Erik?«

»No, it can't. It's a grass snake,« he replied, smiling.

»But a magnificent one, Mama! I found it behind the woods, where the little brook runs into the meadow,« said Jonas, full of pride and admiration; having made such a find was quite an unexpected country pleasure for him, he had only expected caterpillars and at most a slow-worm.

Ruth did not participate in the conversation about the snake, which Jonas could not stop admiring, while they drank coffee. Since they had met Jonas in the garden with the bucket in his hand, Ruth had been completely silent. She had secretly hoped that Klare-Bel would protest against the snake, but she only asked if it could bite anyone to death. And that was the least of what a snake like that could do, thought Ruth.

Now the grass snake managed to stand upright on the bottom of the bucket after several unsuccessful attempts, rhythmically swaying its upper body and looking at the people with its little, smart, black eyes.

Klare-Bel happened to look at Ruth, who was trembling all over, setting down her half-full cup and turning pale.

»Throw that horrid thing away, quickly, Jonas,« his mother said hurriedly, »can't you see Ruth is frightened?«

»No, leave it there,« Erik said calmly, who had been watching Ruth all the time, »no consideration should be given to that.«

Then he turned to her in a light tone: »Liuba told me that you once fainted over a similar trifle. Prove her a liar.«

»Did Liuba say: over a trifle?« Ruth asked, surprised. »It was no trifle. It was something terrible, – cold and creepy, – that came violently from the outside, – like when someone is being killed.«

»For God's sake!« remarked Klare-Bel, »what could that have been?«

»A little caterpillar!« Erik replied mockingly.

Ruth wanted to correct him truthfully: »A big caterpillar,« but it seemed safer to her not to confirm explicitly that it was only a caterpillar.

»Watch out,« cried Jonas, »I will tame this magnificent creature; grass snakes are tame and intelligent, you can wind them around your neck. Then we'll play 'snake charmer.' Have you ever heard anything so wonderful? I am the snake charmer. You don't need to be afraid. You just watch and – and admire me.«

Erik laughed and tousled his short blonde hair.

»Shut your vain mouth,« he warned, »for soon the time will come when Ruth will no longer be content with just watching. When she will voluntarily, on her own initiative, approach the snake, take it in her hand, and let it crawl up her body.«

Ruth had tried in vain to interrupt him.

»Me! When will that be?« she asked, quite beside herself with astonishment.

»When? Probably soon.«

»No! Never!« Ruth assured, still completely stunned by his mistake, »I would always be afraid.«

»Yes, you would. But that's not a counterargument. It happens that one is stronger than one's own fear, and that one overcomes it.«

»Well, Erik, that's a bit much,« said Klare-Bel softly.

Jonas looked puzzled that his father could know something in advance that Ruth herself didn't know yet. But he understood that Erik had predicted something unpleasant for her because she shuddered involuntarily.

»You know what?« Jonas suddenly shouted at her, and the saving idea almost transfigured his face. »I know a way out, – just don't do it! Simply! Just think: you don't have to do it!«

He had to let his parents laugh at him, and the conversation turned to other things.

Ruth sat motionless, looking timidly at the bucket. She was mesmerized by the long, scaly, darting head, which stretched towards her. It seemed to greet her. It seemed to look directly at her. Only her. As if she were alone with the snake.

The little round black eyes seemed to grow larger and larger, like a horrifying abyss where all things uncanny played. And behind the head with the eyes hung the repulsive, slippery creature, writhing impatiently. It was certain: the snake was already lurking for her.

It really did look like it could be up to no good.

Ruth and the grass snake measured each other with their eyes.

Ruth slowly blushed, darker and darker, without saying a word.

Then, as Erik rose from the breakfast table, and Jonas wanted to run back to the garden, Ruth suddenly jumped up and said wildly: »Then right away!«

The others didn't quite understand her, only Erik, who had been watching her closely, let out a sound of surprise.

»Now right away?« he repeated, »no, my child, that's neither good nor necessary. It would be just as much of an exaggeration as working at night. And after this night, you're not strong enough for it.«

»I am strong!« she assured, almost pleading, »but I can't wait for something so terrible! I can't see it creeping up on me – day by day – closer and closer – more and more certain; – living with a snake I'm afraid of, – and becoming more and more intimate with the whole family, – – and it's only lurking for me, – no, I really can't do that!«

Erik laughed but looked concerned. This was quite unwelcome to him.

»But Ruth!« he said, »has your imagination devoured you entirely? Such childish fear is best overcome through gradual acclimatization. I prefer it to happen gradually. Think about it! Because if you insist, there's no turning back! No playing and trying! I wouldn't tolerate that. You must be certain of yourself.«

»Yes!« Ruth claimed, and her forehead became damp.

»Do you still want it? Fine. Then come here.«

Erik observed her with tense attention and simultaneously stepped behind her so that she had to lean back against him if she were to »faint.«

She stood with her arms hanging down, making a determined, almost grim face. But when he reached for the bucket, and she saw the snake writhing in his hand right in front of her, she felt dizzy.

Involuntarily, her hands closed and clenched convulsively, as she commanded them to reach out for the smooth creature; she jerkily closed her eyes, and a buzzing began in her ears.

Then she heard Erik's calm voice: »Are you very afraid?«

She nodded almost imperceptibly.

»Then let's leave it, my child.«

Ruth opened her eyes wide with anticipation.

»Forever?« she asked quickly.

He had to smile.

»No. Not forever,« he said calmly and kindly, »but it's not urgent.«

She pulled herself together.

»Then now right away!« she murmured.

And she stretched out her arm and took the snake from his hand. At the first touch, her whole body shook as if from an electric shock, she threw her head back and pressed herself closer to Erik for support. But her fingers held the long, smooth snake's body tightly, and without uttering a sound, she watched with wide-open eyes as the grass snake stretched itself up her arm, slid around it, and let its head with the fine forked tongue sway to the side.

The arm remained stretched out as if paralyzed. And Ruth made a face as if she were being executed.

»Bravo!« said Erik, who had placed his hands protectively and encouragingly around her, »you did well with this too, girl.«

But when he let go of her and quickly threw the snake back into the bucket, Ruth staggered.

»No, no!« he said cheerfully, »you mustn't think you can 'faint' now. That's no longer an option.« And he pushed a chair toward her.

But Ruth ignored the chair and, without looking up, walked unsteadily past Erik and across the terrace into the hallway. There, as far away from him as possible, she sat down in a corner behind the coat stand, buried her face in the coats hanging there, and began to cry.

Erik watched her in amazement.

»But Ruth, you fool!« he called out and had to laugh, »now you should be happy and even proud. What good is it to cry afterward?«

She peeked out from behind the coat stand and looked at him reproachfully.

»I feel so sorry for myself!« she said and continued to cry.

Jonas, who had stood there with his mouth open the whole time but had kept his growing astonishment to himself at his mother's signal, looked at his father with equal reproach at these words. He ran into the hallway to comfort Ruth.

•

An hour later, Ruth nevertheless went with him and Erik to the city.

The girls at school had long been waiting for her visit. They were extremely interested in the fact that Ruth now lived with Erik, and in every lesson, they asked about her. They found everything had suddenly become so dull. Only a small faction, albeit the best, did not miss Ruth. These were the model students who now felt safe from her antics and were no longer tempted by mischievous ideas. But the mood remained lackluster, and as it began to rain shortly before the holidays, even the most diligent faces turned gloomy.

So, there was great joy when Ruth appeared in the schoolyard during recess, with a big umbrella under which her cheerful face peeked out. Everyone surrounded her, and the noise became so loud that people in the back house looked out of the windows to see what was going on and why the school birds were chirping louder than usual.

Ruth was the only quiet one among them. As she stood there in the middle, surrounded by everyone, it felt as if she had returned from a distant world, and she became almost shy. All the many things she had to tell, all the many things they were eager to hear, melted into a mere look and a smile, and all that remained was the expression of childlike happiness on her face, which spoke for her.

The students squeezed against the wall of the house, where the overhanging roof protected them from the light summer rain, and as back then, when Erik looked down at them from the classroom window, Ruth found her place again on the overturned water barrel.

She seemed changed to the girls, though they couldn't say how. For she still looked like a boy in a blouse among them, and she still hadn't gotten a braid. That she didn't speak escaped them entirely; the accumulated information in them burned on their tongues, and instead of what they wanted to know from her, Ruth learned in a few minutes the fate of each one of them from then until that day, along with the entire course of »public« affairs.

The greatest event they presented to her in person. It was a bride. A real bride from their class. A tall blonde girl with a womanly figure and calm, friendly features. As proof, they slipped a ring from her left hand and triumphantly showed its inscription, – the plain gold wedding band fell into Ruth's lap.

The bride only weakly resisted being treated as communal property. Her thoughts were understandably long out of school, and she felt connected to its inmates only through the immense interest they carried, truly glowing, for her, her beloved, and her happiness. For with her, the whole class considered themselves engaged and married.

»He has dark hair!« explained little blonde Gretchen, who was particularly fond of Ruth, »oh Ruth, such a real fiancé is the highest of all. Just think, what a bride has to tell! When we sit together, and she talks about him and life and marriage and the future, you feel like you learn more in an hour than in all the school years with their stuff.«

»How so?« said Ruth, »she doesn't know anything about it herself.«

Gretchen fell silent, somewhat embarrassed.

»Well, you've become quite prosaic!« another one interjected, laughing, »they love each other after all! Don't you find that wonderful?«

»Yes!« said Ruth, thoughtfully examining the narrow gold ring in her hand; »maybe it's wonderful.« Then she returned it to the bride with a full look and added: »But the wonderful part can't really be told, can it?«

The addressed one blushed slightly and looked at Ruth with joy. For the first time, she felt congratulated on what she possessed entirely for herself, as a bride, – what she couldn't share with the others. »It would have been nicer not to talk so much and so extensively with everyone about it,« she suddenly thought with shame and pride. And while putting the ring back on and looking at Ruth, she couldn't help but think: »This one here is certainly the next bride.«

»Yes, Ruth, you're right: experiencing it might be delightful, telling about it is dull!« cried the pretty dark Wjera in between, who had always been one of the bold ones and now resisted with all her might the dominance of the »brideship« in the class; »you always had such wonderful stories and adventures for us! And now: pure housewife stuff! I'm the only one still chasing the 'noble, unfortunate.'«

»Is he still around?« asked Ruth.

»Yes, just imagine,« someone clapped near Ruth's ear, »she makes actual street acquaintances. There's already been a reprimand.«

»Don't listen to her, Ruth,« interrupted the maligned one, »it's all your fault and your legacy! Why did you stay away with your wonderful recess stories?«

Ruth had leaned her head against the house wall and was looking silently into the rainy courtyard. Right in front of her rose a tall chimney, whose smoke columns blackened the walls year in, year out, and sprinkled their soot onto the schoolyard. Opposite, the massive yellow wall of the back house blocked any view. The air was sultry; she hadn't noticed it outside in the blooming June.

»Like a prison!« thought Ruth and said aloud: »The stories were just a makeshift. Fantasies.«

»How so a makeshift?«

»Would you not tell us any more?«

She shook her head.

»No. No more fantasy stories. Never again. But if you sit in front of a high wall, you naturally imagine what's behind it. And we knew nothing except that there were men behind it. And so, we painted it all with men. You wanted it that way.«

»Well, and what? What else is there behind it?«

»Do you know now what's there?«

»Oh!« said Ruth only, but her eyes opened wide and shone at them all like two unfathomably promising secrets of happiness, »behind it is life.«

In her gaze and expression, there was something so provocative, exciting curiosity and desire, that at that moment even the

»bridegroom« seemed somewhat bland and stale to most. On their faces, it was clear that a new hunger was making itself felt.

»How do you get over the wall?« asked the enterprising Wjera.

Ruth laughed.

»You just climb over,« she said and kept laughing, »and then you go straight, and to the right and to the left, all around and in all directions. Until you're old.«

»Watch out!« warned one of the model students, »don't you see that she's mocking you? She always did that with you. She plays and fantasizes, and then she laughs at us for taking it seriously.«

»Take it seriously!« said Ruth, trying in vain to restrain the imp sitting in her neck.

»So, we should go to Mr. Matthieux and ask him to help us over the wall too?«

»You can do that.«

»He'd probably love and have time for that!«

»He certainly has time,« assured Ruth, »and he has the desire too. He has everything, except the people needed for it.«

They looked at each other with uncertain and smiling glances. And then at Ruth, who sat there indifferently, like embodied comfort.

The tension grew. This seemed to be her best story to them.

»Tell me: is it certain that it's pleasant behind it? Have you never found anything unpleasant there?« asked one of them cautiously.

»Never!« Ruth claimed, and it flashed across her face as she casually remembered that her eyes hadn't been dry since the day before.

The thin-voiced school bell began to ring, and the girls left the place by the fountain.

»You could ask Mr. Matthieux for us,« suggested the pretty Wjera, »it costs nothing.«

»Why?« replied Ruth, »it's your business. Let it cost you something.«

In an excited exchange of opinions, they pushed towards the house. In the excitement she had caused, Ruth herself was forgotten. When the girls then looked around for her to arrange a common way home, Ruth had disappeared. The last thing they heard from her was a laugh.

Erik didn't have as many classes to teach that morning as usual because several private schools had already gone on vacation. So, he came up to his city apartment early, where Ruth was supposed to wait for him. There was still no sign of her. Erik took care of what needed to be done and changed his clothes, glad to escape the hot uniform. When Ruth still didn't show up, he opened the door to the living room, a bit worried, and looked in.

There she lay, sleeping.

She had taken off her little shoes and placed them under a chair. Then she had curled up on the white canvas cover of the sofa with her legs drawn up. Pressing her head against the side cushion, she slumbered with a serious face and sleep-flushed cheeks, fast and earnestly, like a child.

Fatigue must have overtaken her while waiting.

From the gray rainy sky, individual rays of sunlight sneaked through the lowered window curtains, where dust flimmered and shimmered in broad waves, and flitted over Ruth's face. A faint smile glided over her face with the sunbeams and stayed on her lips, like in a dream. Then, as the sun became more insistent, she wrinkled her nose and forehead a few times, and finally, she had to sneeze violently.

Laughter spread across her entire face. Laughing, she woke up and heard Erik laugh.

»Is it morning?« she asked, bewildered, and sat up.

»No. It's noon. Why did you run away from the girls so quickly? They were still asking about you,« he said.

Ruth rubbed her eyes.

»Oh yes, the girls. Now I remember,« she assured, »yes, there's nothing to them. Don't believe it. But it occurred to me: if you can't get living people, – there might be another way.«

»Girl! Shake off the sleep. Are you still dreaming?«

»No, no. Not a dream,« she said eagerly, slipped off the sofa with her feet, propped her arms on the dusty table in front of it, and pressed her chin on her clenched hands; »I thought of it like this: if you want to speak to people, – influence them, – create something great with them, – and you can't find the right people who would fit well, then you have to do it like this: you have to come up with something that you present to them vividly and convincingly, until they get the desire. Can't you do that? Why not? Speak to people about the most beautiful things and don't get tired, – until they get the desire.«

She spoke quickly and animatedly, with wide-awake, shining eyes, visibly trying to make him understand something that seemed to have emerged from her sleep like a dream.

»Who should do that?« he asked slowly, fascinated by her expression, and stepped to the table.

»You should!« she called out brightly, »who else? You always told me: fantasies are useless, but life is beautiful and wide. I believe it! But now I know what fantasy stories are good for, –

because they're good for something. To think up what's still missing in life and add it. To life and people. Isn't that right?«

While she spoke, Erik paced back and forth in the room. It seemed to him that he was listening to the childish expression of what he had only artificially suppressed in himself. It came back and spoke to him with a child's voice. A series of still unclear plans flashed through his mind. Old and new ones mixed together. They had always demanded form. And he, disappointed by circumstances, had tried to push them away, – to forget them. The previous winter, he had thrown himself into a veritable frenzy of social activities to forget them.

Ruth sat and followed him with her eyes. »Now he's certainly thinking of something!« she thought. Several minutes passed in silence.

Neither of them noticed that the air in the room was thick and dusty and that countless gnats were buzzing around.

Then Erik stopped, nodded at her, and said cheerfully: »Thank you, girl. Do you remember that you wanted to give me something that I never really got? Now you've given me something from your fantasy stories after all. At the right time.«

She jumped off the sofa and came to him noiselessly on her stockinged feet.

»Yes,« she said happily, »you wanted to take them out of my head and keep them all for yourself. Only sensible things should go into the head. You said back then: ›Now all your stories are my property, and I can do with them what I want.‹ And now you will do something more beautiful with them than I could.«

She raised her head with an expression of impatient excitement and expectation, then added pleadingly: »But I must be allowed to listen when you come up with something! Can I listen? Will you tell me?«

Erik looked down at her. She seemed so childlike to him, standing there in her stockings. She didn't even reach his shoulder.

Just like in the morning at the desk, he bent down to her, took her face in his hands, and looked into two radiant, happy, pleading child's eyes.

»We will come up with it together!« he said.

•

Klare-Bel had meanwhile had a visitor. When Erik and Ruth came home, a carriage stood at the garden gate. The coachman was turning the light carriage with the English team and letting the horses cool down slowly at a walk.

Warwara Mikhailovna was sitting with Klare-Bel in her small cozy room next to the living room. She had come over from her recently acquired country house, which was about an hour away.

These were usually not just conventional visits that she made to the sick woman. She came gladly, as she was gladly received. She found it soothing with Klare-Bel, because one felt clearly: here lay someone who took real pleasure in hearing about the world outside, the people, and society in a conversational tone. Although she could never return to social activities, she knew them well enough from the first, blissful years of her marriage and still saw them somewhat in the glow of that time. And it was peculiar: when one spoke to such a person, one unconsciously left the worst gossip at home.

Klare-Bel herself never talked much. But Warwara knew that she did not do so with other acquaintances either. She knew: this here was truly a woman who could not be intimate with anyone but her husband.

What Warwara learned about Ruth and her presence in the house fascinated her to the highest degree and almost excited her. But when Ruth then entered the room, she was disappointed.

She had unconsciously expected something striking.

Perhaps a wild, interesting boy in girl's clothing, or perhaps, conversely, a touching, lovely child who shied away, – in any case, something quite unique. Not a pale, well-behaved thing that differed from other young girls only by the polished, assured, and unselfconscious nature of her demeanor towards a stranger.

Ruth, too, was quickly done with Warwara: she took her completely as one of many and presented herself as one among the many that society consists of.

Warwara drew her into conversation a bit and asked where she had been educated.

»I've been to various places,« said Ruth, »but I'm not educated yet.«

It was unclear whether it was meant modestly or boastfully.

»Is she not cunning?« thought Warwara and scrutinized her more closely.

Soon Erik joined them and initiated a cheerful conversation. Warwara talked about the breaking off of an engagement that had just recently been announced. A sensational break, for the bride had fallen in love with another during the short engagement.

Erik, unable to resist the humorous side of the matter, laughed out loud.

Warwara looked over at Ruth. She had gone out.

»By chance? Or a ploy to avoid being sent out during this conversation?« she wondered, »or is she really so childlike that it doesn't interest her?«

After Erik had turned serious again over the two women's saddened faces, he said: »Yes, poor women! When they bind themselves, they have every reason to pray: Dear God, help me to be a good wife. For their only protection against themselves lies, indeed, in the continued, purely emotional nature of their love, – in actual emotional fidelity. They can also hold on out of a sense of duty, but that's a stunted life.«

»You mean, a man doesn't need such a prayer,« remarked Warwara, not hiding her irony.

He looked at her quite unaffectedly. »No,« he said, »I believe a man is better protected in this point, as in so many others, by his nature. Not against infidelity of the senses. Not against the change of love. But against the conscious inner letting go of the being he has bound himself to, – no: the being he has bound to himself. That's the point!«

»That's original. You attribute a strength of duty consciousness, a nobility of compassion to the man, which we, – the women, – do not –«

»Oh no, don't get upset. No sense of duty, just a greater awareness of happiness than you have. No compassionate nobility, just a possessive pride that you lack. The man who takes a woman for himself and upon himself forever enjoys, alongside the joy of love, another specific male pleasure: he consciously lays his hand on this whole being that belongs to him and says: 'Mine.' To him, his happiness through the woman means three things: being able to love, – wanting to take responsibility, – being allowed to rule.«

Warwara shuddered.

»God preserve your arrogance!« she said, »but for me, the idea that the woman is the man's queen is much more appealing.«

»You see, – – I say even more: his kingdom,« he said with a smile, »that's why she gives him up sooner than he gives her up. For her, there is rebellion, insurrection, revolution against him,

– all of which can look quite heroic and very enticing. For the man, however, giving up his own kingdom would be something that would go against his sense of shame.«

Warwara laughed in his face.

»And this is you, who so gladly advocates all sorts of modern development struggles, and also for those of women,« she cried, »it's a dreadful inconsistency and self-deception on top of that! For if you were to fall in love with such a developed future woman, who no longer thinks so medievally, and you couldn't subdue her?«

»But I would!« said Erik. »Otherwise, I might be enthusiastic about her, admire her, support her, respect her as a comrade in the fight, – but love her, – how could I? As little as if she were a woman, or she were a sexless being. I can imagine a man completely relinquishing all desire to rule for the sake of a cause he places above himself. In love – never! And a woman who doesn't cater to this instinct – doesn't work as a woman.«

»And this contradiction is supposed to lie in nature itself? No, only in your centuries-old nurtured arrogance,« retorted Warwara indignantly and turned to Klare-Bel: »What do you say to such a man? We should place ourselves under the man for all future if we love?«

Klare-Bel replied somewhat uncertainly: »I think we do it not because we stand below him, but because we want to be happy.«

All three began to laugh. Warwara stood up to go home.

»Now I should have had enough of this,« she remarked cheerfully to Erik, »but from my little niece at the girls' school, I learned that you will be giving the usual grand speech at the upcoming school closing ceremony. I'll be there. So you know: One will be sitting there mocking you. And it will certainly sound nice. I've always enjoyed your toasts at social gatherings.«

Erik had to laugh.

»You shouldn't remind me so forcibly that our most beautiful speeches are taken as toasts,« he replied, »and that almost the only attentive listeners we can find besides the schoolchildren are the bored beautiful women of our superficial society.«

»Dearest, you are a witness that I have to take my revenge,« Warwara said, offended, to Klare-Bel, »I'd just like to know if it wouldn't hurt you if the beautiful women all stayed away. I believe, then this barbarian would carry you on his back and set you among his schoolchildren, who all fear him like fire.«

»That will probably never happen,« Klare-Bel said somewhat sadly.

»Oh yes! No one can foresee the future. We will now conduct a treatment of my wife based on a consultation with the professor, which promises wonders,« Erik said to Warwara and escorted her to her carriage.

•

Jonas came home later than Erik and Ruth and only appeared when the visit had left and they were already sitting at the table.

He had spent the meantime in the farthest corner of the garden under the dripping trees, wrestling with a great decision. His grass snake was with him, hanging melancholically around his neck, as if it already knew something very unpleasant awaited it. Once more he had lovingly taken it in his arms, petted it, and pressed it tenderly to him, once more he had reveled in its precious possession. Then he had killed it.

To do it, he had to muster courage and harden his heart. He had to imagine himself as a new Hercules, rescuing Hesione from a sea monster, or even better, as Perseus, conquering Andromeda. But this image didn't quite work. His poor grass snake didn't look like a sea monster at all, Ruth just misunderstood it. The creature looked at him with such lively little eyes, and he loved it so much.

Then an old fairy tale crossed his mind, comforting him, about a snake with a golden crown on its head; whoever killed it, it turned into a charming princess. He couldn't remember exactly if that was how it went, but he liked it. And his princess was certainly already waiting for him.

After Jonas had committed the murder, he turned toward the house with a red face. It was a huge sacrifice, he thought, that they had made for Ruth, he and the grass snake. For the snake remained dead, and he had been as excited about it as about a riding horse.

And now Ruth kept talking at the table about those silly schoolgirls he couldn't stand. It annoyed him that she had run to the recess with them today because until now, he had been her only playmate, and in this regard, Jonas was not amused.

They were still at lunch when a courier arrived and handed Erik a telegram.

He opened it and scanned the contents, then pushed his plate back and stepped to the window with the paper. One could see it was joyful and moving news.

»Almost a whole letter! Sent from the border,« he said, »imagine, Bel, my old friend Bernhard Römer is on his way here. Seventeen years we haven't seen each other. Or even longer? Back then we were still students! Do you remember him?«

»Oh yes, Erik! How could I forget him! Because with him, you always made such grand plans for the future. You wanted to turn everything upside down. Yes, you were so young back then. What has Römer become?«

»He's a professor of medicine at Heidelberg University. He still wrote to me sometimes in earlier years.«

Ruth had stopped eating and looked at Erik with wide eyes. With the change in his expression and Klare-Bel's words, it seemed to Ruth that a completely foreign and distant past was suddenly rising between them. A past where she had not been present. Not even in the world! It seemed quite impossible to her.

»Will he come here?« she asked quietly.

»Unfortunately not. He's just passing through. His destination is Moscow. There's some medical conference there. I'll find out more at the train station tomorrow morning. Did he bring his wife?«

»To a medical conference?« doubted Klare-Bel.

»Why not? I believe they are closely intertwined in their intellectual life. Römer married very young, his wife went through his entire storm and stress period with him. That gave their whole marriage its character.«

»Don't they have children?« Klare-Bel asked, as this point particularly interested her.

»I don't think so.«

»No children!« repeated Klare-Bel in a tone of regret. Nothing in her suffering seemed as hard to her as the fact that she could not become a mother again. »That's a sad marriage, just the two of them.«

»As far as I remember, they haven't always lived just the two of them. They have repeatedly taken in young girls who studied at the university.«

»Young girls studying at the university? Can they do that there?« Ruth asked, astonished.

Erik looked at her with a smile.

»Indeed. Young girls like you,« he said; »there's nothing to stop you from becoming one of Römers' next house children. Would you like that?«

He said it jokingly, but the look with which she answered him was so serious that it stayed in his memory.

Erik sat back at the table and chatted with his wife about old times. Jonas thought now Ruth could go out with him, but she remained seated and listened.

Outside, it had begun to rain harder. Jonas leaned against the house door on the terrace and looked out thoughtfully. When Ruth finally got up from the lunch table and went into the hallway, he remarked: »If we could at least play 'man and wife' in rainy weather. It's so suitable for indoors. Because when the sun shines, you don't do it. And then it's also something you can't have with your silly girls.«

»Oh yes!« Ruth assured and swung onto the railing of the narrow wooden staircase leading up to her attic room, »we often played that in the schoolyard.«

»That must have been a fine arrangement without a real boy!« Jonas said disdainfully. »And I would much rather be your husband than the man in all those robber stories where I always have to exert myself.«

»But I don't want to be your wife,« she said coldly, sitting there and swinging her legs, »and then that would be even more strenuous for you. Be glad that you're always the main character and the hero.«

»No, you always are!« he accused her sulkily.

»No, Jonas, that's definitely not true. You're the main character all by yourself. Weren't you Egmont just yesterday? And recently —«

»Yes, at the beginning!« he interrupted her irritably, »but if you always have to tell me everything in advance and possibly even act it out, then I'm not really it, only you.«

»I can't help it if you're dumb.«

Jonas fell silent, hurt. If she only knew whom she was saying that to; – if she only knew that he had voluntarily refrained from showing her his superiority, scaring her, making her beg and flatter! Because if they had played 'snake charmer,' he would have been the master. And she was so foolish to believe him that the snake had really escaped.

Jonas was burning to tell Ruth about his sacrifice. But he thought his pride as a man forbade him. He would rather bite his tongue off if the urge to gossip became too great.

»If I was Egmont, then you should have been my Klärchen,« he said; »were you?«

»No, of course not. I didn't get around to it. Because alone you wouldn't have managed to bring him out. And he's the most important, as you can imagine. Klärchen can be left out.«

»But I have no desire to be your puppet! Be my wife!« he shouted angrily and stamped his foot.

Ruth had slipped off the railing. She stood by the low hallway window, against which the rain was trickling, and pressed her face flat against the pane, distorting it satyr-like. When Jonas got furious, his voice always cracked: it wavered between too high and too deep. That always made Ruth laugh.

Then Jonas tore his cap from the coat rack and stormed out.

»Run to your silly girls!« he shouted angrily, »I'm a boy!«

In the end, Ruth might not be the ideal woman he needed. Andromeda had agreed to follow her rescuer as a slave through all lands. Ruth would never do something like that, it wouldn't even occur to her, – he was firmly convinced of that.

From the terrace, Jonas stuck his head through the open living room window and asked if he could visit a friend until evening tea.

Klare-Bel, who was lying beside the cleared table and reading van Lennep's novellas, looked up at his words.

»It's good that he still thinks of such things,« she remarked after his head had disappeared from the window, »because now he thinks day and night only of the girl, Erik.«

»A flash in the pan!« he replied.

He stood and looked dreamily out. His thoughts still lingered in the past. His wife took the next day only as a welcome distraction and was happy about it for him. For him, it was more than that.

»Do you think it doesn't harm him?« Klare-Bel asked worriedly. »But you said yourself Jonas has become careless and distracted in his studies.«

»That he is a bit. But what he may lack in book learning, he regains a thousandfold in the happy stimulation that invigorates and rouses his mental powers. No school can replace that.«

»He's still like a child. But Jonas is affectionate. If he now attaches his heart so entirely to her –?«

»Then let him have the memory of meeting Ruth. He can attach it to nothing better, Bel.«

She remained silent at that. The Dutch novella book slipped from her hands. She folded them in her lap.

»How highly he esteems her!« she thought secretly, startled.

•

The next day was a quiet one. Because Erik didn't come home. The house seemed deserted without the sound of his steps and voice.

He probably wouldn't return until the last night train, Bel thought. He surely wouldn't like to leave her alone in the country at night.

Jonas crept around the house in a foul mood. After yesterday's quarrel, he felt a strong urge for a thorough reconciliation followed by inseparable togetherness. But Ruth wasn't up for that today. She had completely forgotten the quarrel. And to all his suggestions for doing something together, she responded only with her well-known stereotypical: »I need to think.«

And Jonas already knew that she was as good as lost to him then.

Ruth continued thinking, incessantly about the same thing. In her thoughts, she followed Erik to the city, to the train that was to bring him his friend, and tried to immerse herself in the reunion.

When Klare-Bel called out to him in the morning as he left: »Goodbye, Erik, have a good time!« Ruth had almost looked up, startled. It seemed to her as if Erik was about to undertake something so serious and moving. Even his face seemed changed to her since yesterday. Beneath everything he spoke or did in the usual way, Ruth sensed that a whole world of stirred memories was constantly whispering and talking in him. Not memories that amused, – but ones that forcibly pulled back into a past, casting a shadow over the present.

Today the garden lay in friendly sunshine. Klare-Bel's chair had been moved to the terrace; she couldn't stay downstairs because Erik wasn't there to carry her back up. A warm summer scent rose from outside; lilacs and laburnum were fading, and the roses on the beds were opening. Tree tops and bushes now pressed so closely together that it was almost too much foliage and shade around the house. The summer now completely enclosed it in its warm darkness, and seen from the road, the garden looked like a big green blot.

When evening tea was drunk on the terrace, Klare-Bel noticed that Ruth sat there, seemingly absent-minded.

»It's almost as if she can't stand Erik being occupied with other people anymore; she would prefer to deny him any distraction, this wicked little egoist,« she thought and asked aloud: »But child, are you missing something? What kind of strange look do you have? I think you would rather be there with Erik?« Ruth caught the not entirely kindly tone with her fine ear and looked at her timidly.

»I'm trying to be there!« she said to Klare-Bel's unspeakable astonishment.

She soon retired to her small room to rest early, feeling somewhat unwell. Perhaps the new treatment Erik had recently started for her was affecting her, and it was supposed to continue for several months. He really was beginning to draw new hope.

Gonne left after carefully bedding her down, and Klare-Bel lay alone in her quiet room, surrounded by all the dainty and neat little things she liked to keep around her.

She lay there and smiled at herself. Hadn't it recently felt as if she was also gently – secretly nurturing the new hope? Just a little. The hope of getting well again, of being able to walk out to meet Erik on two healthy feet.

Of course, there was nothing to it. A mere delusion. But if it deceived, Erik would carry her over it, just like over the many, many earlier disappointments. Because that's what he had done, – not with excessive pity and protection, but with his constant presence, with his continuous energetic influence on her. And sometimes she distinctly felt: it was good so because he needed it; only in this effort did he overcome his own disappointments. His strong influence on others seemed to be what always brought him back to his old confidence. So often had she observed it with wonder in daily life among the people of his former surroundings, how invigorating it was for him that they expected strength and animation from him. Erik truly could not tolerate being alone.

Time advanced, and Klare-Bel still lay awake, dreaming with open eyes. Through the open window, the air brushed softly and moistly, carrying whole swarms of small gnats; in the distance, the song of the last farmworkers returning home from their nightly work faded quietly. With bright sunlit eyes, the night looked into the room.

Klare-Bel's thoughts were rebellious and even exuberant, astonishing herself. »Who is strong,« she thought, »if the strong one needs the weak?« She was certainly a weak being, glad if Erik wanted to take her by the hand and lead her. But he, didn't he need someone around him whom he could lead, to be happy and sure of his path? Did Erik need her as she needed him?

Klare-Bel smiled in the solitude of the bright night, and her longing stretched out to him fervently.

•

As she had expected, Erik set off for home much later. He had accompanied his friend to the Moscow train station with many others, and then they had spent some more time together, – a whole bunch of people, strangers and acquaintances, with whom the evening was spent in lively sociability. Erik no longer took the time to drive home to change; he barely caught the last night train and headed out to the country.

The long walk from the station did him good after the past hours and impressions; the fresh night air revived him. Not a breath of air stirred, the almost daylight sky was pale and glitterless with the full moon, individual clouds piled up, and from time to time, a fine rain sprinkled down.

When he arrived at the house, lying bright under the motionless trees in the night, the still excited mood slowly gave way to a feeling of quiet joy at being home again, with his own. With his own! Ruth now belonged there too. Belonged to him.

He climbed the steps to the terrace quietly and glanced at the attic room where she was now sleeping and dreaming. Then, as he had unlocked the front door almost noiselessly, the narrow wooden staircase leading up from the hallway creaked under a light foot. Completely dressed, only her hair a bit disheveled around her head, Ruth appeared on the bottom step.

»But Ruth, what are you thinking? How could you stay up? Quickly to bed!« he said.

He scolded, but it sounded very heartfelt. Her dear face felt like a welcome greeting to him.

»Was it nice?« she asked, looking at him with wide, awake eyes, »should I have slept through it? No, I couldn't! because I was there too, – always there. Was it nice?«

He reached for her outstretched hand and held it tight. All the impressions of the day, all the memories they had stirred up, vanished; he had left the entire stream of people behind and was only with her.

What did all the stimulation mean to him, indeed, what all the so long desired applause or success, for which he had strived and fought in life, compared to the delicate praise that spoke from Ruth's childish, believing devotion to him? How bland and brutal appeared everything that came from a crowd and expressed itself loudly. Only those whose senses had become too dull for such fine fragrance might seek sharper spices.

This thought flew through Erik's mind, and in the process, he forgot to answer.

He looked handsome in his formal attire, the wide coat loosely thrown over him, rain-sprinkled, and above it his animated face.

As they stood there facing each other in the silent night, while the whole world around them was asleep, they both appeared saturated with life, and something related seemed to speak from both expressions, – related beyond age and gender, – a life-demanding, life-asserting quality. It was the same that had touched Erik so familiarly and deeply when he first saw Ruth in the schoolyard, with mischief in her eyes and raised arms.

They stood and remained silent, and around them, the magical brightness in which evening and morning imperceptibly blended together dreamed.

»Shouldn't I have gone, Ruth?« he asked involuntarily, looking at her with a smile.

»Yes! But take me with you!« she replied, and in the sound of her voice, the whole longing and self-entrancement in which she had spent the day revealed itself. Erik didn't fully understand her; he took the subsequent request more childishly and factually than Ruth meant it, but look, tone, and demeanor expressed so clearly that she had felt lost during his absence that a deep emotion came over him.

To him, Ruth looked enchanted, – different, more lovely than usual.

The house remained completely still, and they spoke in low voices. Only through the open door to the house came a soft, mysterious whispering and rustling, – a murmuring that passed through the low bushes outside, – the first announcement of the new day.

»It's time!« said Erik, startled, »go to bed. Good night! Good morning, darling!«

And with a quick movement, he pulled her to him – tightly, so that she lay against his chest, and kissed her on the mouth.

As he let her go just as quickly, Ruth took his hand and pressed her warm lips to it.

Then she flew up the narrow steps to her attic room.

Erik opened the middle door in the hallway, which led to Jonas's room. He had to pass through it to reach his bedroom behind. Jonas woke up.

»Well, Dad, was it nice?« he asked, turning sleepily to the other side; »was there champagne too?«

With that, he went back to sleep.

Erik opened a window and looked out into the bright distance. A colorless, pale, even gray spread through the room, and the dawning morning began to fill it with harsh cold.

The gentle rustling and whispering no longer crept along the ground but had risen higher. It moved the branches of the wild acacias standing close to the window and then swelled mightily until it resounded majestically through the old treetops that had previously stood silently against the bright night sky.

It sounded like a morning hymn, and – very quietly, – tentatively, as if still half-asleep, a small, cheerful bird call occasionally fell in. And soon after, like an exultation, a long, tireless chaffinch trill.

Erik had gone to bed but with wakeful, listening senses, he absorbed the approach of the day, and it seemed to him like a suitable accompaniment to his thoughts, which still lingered on Ruth. For they, too, bore a delicate and half-veiled mood, a morning dream mood, it seemed to him.

Never before had he been so deeply moved by the feeling that they irrevocably belonged to each other, that they were fundamentally of the same nature, the same essence. And only now did he seem to understand her plea: »Take me with you!« What he was, she wanted to be too, for only in him did she grasp and sense herself. The same life force slumbered strongly and joyfully in both of them. Only in her did it spring from an unconscious, untouched natural ground, what in him had been conscious decision, reason, and will. And only in her did it still burn with a pure flame, what in him the touch with life had already mixed with slag and ashes.

And over this unclear thought, Erik began to dream.

The first jubilation of the birds outside subsided, and the morning wind fell silent. Like them, the old trees stood motionless against the sky, through whose blue scattered white clouds floated. In a broad stream of gold, the sunlight flooded the room.

Behind Erik's closed eyelids, it painted smiling rosy colors. He fell asleep in the sunshine.

IV.

Short and scorching as always, the Russian midsummer had flown by, and early, in the middle of August, autumn quietly settled in the garden, extinguishing the sun with its long, dark evenings. The lawn looked pale and scorched, and the first dry leaves gathered along the gravel paths.

Right where Klare-Bel lay in her chair at the edge of the small grove, she could look up through the birch branches above her into a broad, golden-yellow patch that grew a little larger each day. From time to time, one of the discolored leaves would fall, spin a few times in the air, and flutter down to her.

Next to her stood a table, roughly made from unpeeled tree branches, and two benches with backrests made from a coarse wickerwork of willow twigs. There, Erik and Ruth had been sitting and working for half the day.

Klare-Bel couldn't understand how they could endure it so continuously; sometimes it seemed to her that they were only having conversations, but she knew how seriously they took it and that Erik sometimes stayed up all night preparing his lessons.

She liked lying there and listening, not to the words, but to the voices. For she did not deceive herself: only in these hours did Erik's voice sound as joyful as it used to. And it was truly good that he now almost avoided his room and always sat with Ruth nearby, where she could hear him.

Often she thought back with secret worries and doubts to the first day in June, which Erik had spent in the city with Bernhard Römer and his wife. Since the following morning, he had been changed. And it had to be connected to that day. But she sought the true reason in the distant past, especially since she had seen the mutual friend from their youth again.

For since then, she quite understood that Erik might still quietly follow old memories. Even her own thoughts returned more frequently than ever to where there was no return.

Youth does not rise again.

If only there were a joy, she thought secretly to herself, a great, powerful joy that she could bring into Erik's life, so that he would forget everything over it! But she possessed nothing, – she had always just lain there with empty hands and borne sacrifices.

A few days ago, Erik had unexpectedly brought out the professor, whom he sometimes consulted for her treatment. She had been laid on her bed, and then Erik had held her tightly in his arms, trembling with fear and pain, until the agonizing minutes were over. He himself was very pale. But the professor wanted to come back.

»Does it have to be, Erik?« she asked timidly.

»It has to be. There is a change,« he replied evasively.

Change! Perhaps recovery!

Yes, there could only be one great, powerful joy left: if she herself rose from her bed and stepped to him on her own feet, – then he must become happy again.

And wistfully, Klare-Bel looked into the sunlit golden-green branches, from which the leaves slowly fell. And her thoughts wandered.

As the rays of the afternoon sun fell more obliquely and the shadows of the trees began to lengthen and stretch, the two at the table fell silent, and Ruth stood up.

During these lessons, it seemed peculiar to Klare-Bel each time that it was always Ruth who decided when to end. Erik wanted it that way: only she herself could know exactly when her full freshness and receptivity diminished. For his part, he could only put all his undivided strength into what he gave her, – and that he did. He gathered all the forces of will and mind and concentrated them on a single point: he held Ruth like a princely child, to be gifted only with the finest.

He looked at her as she stood beside him, sun-tanned and with her hair blown forward, in a proper Russian peasant blouse of coarse unbleached linen, with red embroidery on the shoulder pieces and upper sleeves, – almost like a child of the people. But she was his princely child.

He had pulled over a notebook without intending to look through it; his eyes merely glided mechanically over the lines. But Ruth stayed beside him, and now she leaned over him to look in. Erik grew more nervous by the second. And suddenly, he reprimanded her so harshly for a minor mistake he found that Klare-Bel looked up in shock.

Ruth raised her shoulders and eyebrows and shook her head indignantly.

»It's unbelievable. How can one be so mindless, – isn't it? One must be downright stupid for that!« she continued his reproaches with undisguised self-contempt.

Erik was taken aback and had to laugh at her.

But it touched him strangely. Just a few months ago, something like this would have made her shy, – would have scared her off. Now she no longer cried over being called a stupid child by him. She laughed. Laughed at herself. – Her eyes looked at him so mockingly. Who was she actually mocking? Herself, – there was no doubt about that. She took herself as an object, which she only judged from Erik's perspective; she felt, thought, and acted only as if from his being.

What was this self-removal, this excess of self-forgetfulness at its core? Was it love? Was it what he, only half-consciously and against his will, – was waiting for?

Klare-Bel had laughed along.

»It will seem strange to you,« she said, »when you get so many fellow learners with Erik in the fall. When you have to share everything with them. Won't you be jealous then if one of the girls knows more than you?«

»Why?« asked Ruth, and the mischief glinted in her eyes, »then we'll like that one better than me. We have room for many here. The more there are, the better.«

Erik looked up. Would she really welcome a third party into their bond with enthusiasm? But when she looked so roguishly, no one could know what she was thinking to herself.

He got up and pushed his wife's chair towards the house to carry her inside before sunset. Jonas came towards them; he had been roaming the mown meadows all afternoon, but he always timed the moment right when he could claim Ruth.

When Erik came out of the house again, he saw Ruth walking back and forth under the birches with Jonas. They held each other loosely, nudging each other towards the grassy edge where the early autumn had piled up the withered leaves. They apparently took lively pleasure in rustling through the leaves with their feet.

Jonas had taken Ruth's hand, which lay on his shoulder, and from time to time, he tilted his head sideways and caressed his cheek with her hand.

»Jonas!« Erik called out loudly to the boy.

He started at the tone.

»What should I do?« he asked, coming closer sheepishly.

»You should work on your holiday assignments!« said Erik, ashamed of himself.

Ruth followed Jonas into the house.

Erik remained standing in the garden, watching the two.

There it was again, – this childish, childlike, this immature and strangely unripe aspect in Ruth's nature. It didn't diminish, it increased, – it was deeply rooted somewhere, in the core of her being. Intellectually, she had developed quickly and strongly, like young leaves in the warm May rain. But it seemed as if now all the childlike elements were also developing and pushing for fuller expression, – and alongside them, others, almost masculine, which he had only suspected in her until now. She quickly got used to shaping her thoughts with logical precision and giving them a vigorous direction towards understanding, as if she had never lived in the fantasy of dreams. Clearly, the entangled, unclear, and wildly rambling nature of her thinking was only connected to the fantastic subjects themselves and fell away with them.

Erik slowly walked back into the house, where Jonas sat in the living room with a resigned expression over his books, seemingly studying; but secretly, he was pondering how to win Ruth away from his father to have her more to himself. Tomorrow was a Sunday, so much could be done; during these vacation months, they ate early, so they got a long afternoon and evening out of it. But Jonas found it unfair that there were only one Sunday for six weekdays and that the father had claimed the weekdays.

Ruth was not in the living room. She must have gone up to her little attic room.

Erik went back to the hallway and listened for any movement upstairs.

And then he was already at the foot of the narrow wooden staircase.

He felt like a thief as he hesitated on the bottom step in the half-dusk.

Slowly, he took the first steps, then quickly the next.

How long it had been since he had been alone with Ruth, – completely alone. – –

Upstairs, he knocked shortly and loudly. Ruth answered in a bright voice. She stood in front of the open wardrobe, where her things were stored, rummaging through them.

Besides a table and chair by the window, the small room didn't contain much more than on the first day. But the windowsill was filled with flowers, common summer flowers like those carried by street vendors on a headboard, and on the floor were pots with cuttings from the garden. And the wallpaper was covered with pencil drawings, all framed with a broad ink border. They all came from Jonas's hand and depicted various corners of the garden or the house.

Erik looked down at the table where sewing materials and papers were scattered in disarray.

It didn't occur to Ruth to ask why he had come up, but in his own slight embarrassment, he searched for words and pulled one of the papers out from under the sewing materials.

»Are you writing verses here?« he asked, surprised.

She turned dark red.

»Not so often anymore,« she replied, almost startled, »and I don't want to! But sometimes, if – – sometimes I still have to.«

»So, you do hidden things. Hidden from me. And I believed that no thought went unspoken through your head that I didn't know.«

She made such a shy face like in old times.

»Not hidden,« she said quietly, »they just aren't thoughts. And they can't be spoken. And they come and insist, and then you have to write verses.«

Erik laughed.

»Oh dear, the poor verses!« he remarked. »So you've reserved such a quiet corner in your head, while it looks like you've made the best order. That's probably only in the state rooms, on the surface. But behind that, there's a beautiful, unfathomable junk room. What should we do with that?«

She looked at him quite seriously.

»Whatever you want,« she replied sincerely.

»Would you unquestioningly do what I want? Even in the secret, what you do for yourself? Even in the most hidden part of your junk room? Always?«

»Always.«

He took her head between his hands.

»And if I wanted to clear it out for you? And if it happened to be your favorite corner? And if someday, perhaps, it was no longer just a junk room but your happy mental home? Would you still answer the same way: 'Whatever you want'?«

»Yes!« she said simply.

Erik made a gesture as if he wanted to pull her into his arms, then he let her go, stepped back and to the window, next to which a small bookshelf hung on the sidewall.

A few minutes passed.

Ruth watched him as he apparently studied the titles of the books, which were no longer visible in the slowly increasing dusk. But Erik roughly knew what had come together here in the strangest harmony. A Latin grammar from Jonas's legacy and the fairy tales of One Thousand and One Nights, a selection from Plato's works in German translation and a torn volume of old Russian folk tales, Überweg's "System of Logic" and the French translation of Don Quixote with Doré's illustrations, and so on.

»Why have you never written a book?« Ruth suddenly asked from the window.

»Because I never could. I don't understand writing books, Ruth. And it always seemed to me: books are dead, only the spoken word lives. And I fear you'll never be able to either, never understand, my poor girl.«

»Me? I don't want to either. I want something else.«

»What do you want?«

»Tell a fairy tale. Just one. One in which everything is included. But not with words.«

»You would have to write or speak, paint or sculpt it if you want to share it.«

»There must be a better way,« said Ruth.

»Not if it's meant for everyone. Otherwise, you might as well read it in a dear person's eyes.«

»That's better,« she said and leaned her head back against the window frame.

Both were silent for a short time.

The twilight sank deeper. On the stone tiles of the terrace below, it blinked brightly, the lamp was lit in the living room.

Around the top of the old elm tree outside the window, the bats played. Silently, they darted from under the roof and fluttered back and forth behind Ruth's back in a zigzag.

Erik suddenly stood close to her in the half-dark. He lifted his hands and gently ran them through her hair, so that they got lost in the soft, curly waves, and then they rested on her shoulders, and he bent deeply over Ruth.

»Don't say that to me again, – what you said earlier: that you would always and unquestioningly do what I want,« he remarked in a low voice, »you shouldn't follow me blindly in every case. – I could want something wrong from you too. – Haven't you thought of that?«

She leaned back far into his arm and shook her head.

He held her tighter.

»And if it were so?« he asked almost fiercely, »what would you do?«

Only now did Ruth look up and gaze at him long and calmly. She seemed to seriously consider the situation.

»Do wrong!« she said loudly.

Erik recoiled. He murmured something she didn't understand. But she laughed all over her face.

»For me, whatever you want is always right, – never wrong. I don't need to know better. I don't need to know better.«

»My poor child,« he said softly.

She straightened up in his arm. A listening expression came over her face.

»Who? Me? Why do you say that?« she asked with a changed voice and slowly freed herself. »What is this? Why are you telling me all this? I'm not a poor child. I'm your child!«

And when he didn't answer immediately, she suddenly grabbed him by both arms and shook them with passionate strength. »Am I not?« she asked wildly. »Why shouldn't I do what you want? Am I not your child? Not anymore?! Then it would be better to be dead.«

»Ruth!« he called, shaken.

She tried to collect herself. Her hands dropped from his arms and intertwined. Then she raised her head.

»I'll do everything, – everything! Right or wrong, good and bad, – everything! I will be obedient unto death. Test me. But I must be allowed to obey you, – be your child, – be allowed to say to you: I will do what you want. Always! Always! I must – I must be allowed. – – May I?«

Unconsciously, she raised her clasped hands slightly. A gesture of unspeakable humility. But her face looked almost grim, and her voice sounded like metal. And only at the end, a very soft, childish tone: »– May I?«

Erik felt as if he was suddenly looking, for the first time in these fleeting seconds, into the hidden depths from which Ruth's love could be born. For the first time into the mystery of her being, – into the silent loneliness and longing of many, many years, from which the long-restrained, long-stored fervor had broken out with unrestrained force when he entered her life. To be allowed to love him meant: finally – finally to be allowed to be a child, to obey, to give oneself away, – even on one's knees. It meant to gather and pour out all the passionate tenderness of a child who has never had a childhood. And who needed just that – only that.

Ruth's eyes flashed at him through the twilight.

»Am I still poor, – a poor child?« they seemed to ask him unblinkingly.

»You are not poor, – you are my child, – and you may obey, – follow me, – you shall always be allowed to,« he said hoarsely.

And he opened the door to the staircase, where the lamp light shone brightly from the hallway below.

- •

That evening, Erik retired to his study immediately after tea. Klare-Bel noticed very well that he stayed up half the night again. Although there was no lesson the next day.

The next morning, at the breakfast table, Erik asked if there were any letters to take to the city.

»Are you going to the city? Today? On a Sunday?« his wife asked uneasily.

»Yes, I have to take care of two urgent letters and make a necessary visit,« he replied.

She saw the two letters on the side table. One to Römer in Heidelberg, the other to his wife in Moscow. Both doubly stamped.

She didn't dare to ask him what he had to write so much to Mrs. Römer about? He looked so dismissive, so closed off. But after he had left, Klare-Bel spent the whole morning sadly and worriedly thinking about his face.

This reticent, closed-off demeanor she knew as a bad sign. Erik was open and communicative when he was happy; when he was silent, he suffered. And just then, Klare-Bel would have liked to share everything with him. Faced with the happy, the cheerful, she always felt a little pressured, a little superfluous. On the other hand, suffering and sorrow always seemed to her the most suitable ways to access Erik's inner self, which she should have found too, – to get close to him, to become necessary to him. But just when he suffered, he became the most inaccessible, – always rejecting to the point of brusqueness. Only in his joyful hours did he open up to her.

So it was probably nothing for her: neither with the joy she wanted to bring him so much, – nor with the sorrow she would have borne with him.

Meanwhile, Erik was in the city at Ruth's relatives' house. Contrary to his expectation, he found the aunt at home, who had just returned from Wiesbaden and was to travel to Livonia shortly, where her husband was to accompany her.

»We won't be back until before winter,« the uncle said to Erik, whom he warmly welcomed again and only after a long, informal conversation, led into the drawing-room to his wife. »But all you told me doesn't have to be rushed, I think. If you carry out your plan to send Ruth abroad, we could coordinate the timing of our return a bit, couldn't we?«

»No!« replied Erik, »what I wanted to ask of you was just this: to give me completely free hand in this as well. And to stick to the travel arrangement I have in mind for Ruth. Even if that should accelerate her departure unpredictably. I know I'm asking a lot of you. But if you have confidence in me, then let me decide about Ruth once more, as unconditionally as when I first took her away from you.«

»I don't know any person in the wide world in whom I could place more trust than in you,« said Ruth's uncle, whose coziness vanished with Erik's peculiar tone, »and as far as Ruth is concerned, I've always had the feeling from the beginning that even such close relatives as we are must yield you a right to the girl. So, if you firmly believe it's good for her, then act so! I, for my part, will – if I don't see her again – take a short leave at Christmas and visit our little student in Heidelberg.«

»But please! Don't call it by the worst name!« the aunt interjected, finding her husband's leniency irresponsible. »Ruth isn't really supposed to study, is she? I mean with a student plaid and short hair, as they do here? In our Baltic provinces, such a thing would be purely unthinkable.«

»For the time being, she's to learn,« Erik replied somewhat dismissively, »we will leave the rest to her and time.«

She looked at him critically and disapprovingly. How could one leave such a thing to »time«? If he had at least said »providence«. If he supported women's studies, then he was certainly an atheist. And such people were indeed capable of anything.

»I see with astonishment that my husband thinks very carelessly about this,« she remarked as Erik stood up to say goodbye, »but I must add a word. You speak so calmly of yielding rights, Louis! But a right you can never, ever yield. I mean the right of moral responsibility. That may be an old-fashioned view. But I'd like to know what Mr. Matthieux thinks about it.«

Erik looked her seriously and calmly in her combative eyes. For the first time, he liked her. It was the combativeness that pleased him. Though the uncle loved Ruth, she was a better guardian than he.

»If I understand you correctly,« he said, »you fear that I would not also take on all the duties towards Ruth with my right to her. If there's anything that can free you from this fear, name it to me.«

The uncle looked almost embarrassed, but she didn't notice it.

»I answer you as a believing woman,« she replied, proud of her Baltic conviction, »for me, moral responsibility means: being willing to be guilty for a person, – guilty of what happens to their inner being. Not allowing them to suffer harm. How should one be able to take that on without God, without religious faith? If you now send Ruth away, – can you take on such a duty in this sense?«

A look passed over Erik's features, which she couldn't interpret, but which moved her against her will.

»Now we understand each other,« he said with suppressed emotion, »for that is precisely what I want my right to be: I want to be guilty for this child!«

She found it sounded more arrogant than ever. It wasn't anything that could soothe her religious concerns. But still, she felt as if he had said »God«.

Erik walked to the station. Almost no one else was on the empty streets; even the last ones who had to spend the summer in the hot, unhealthy swamp air of the city had escaped it on Sunday. Only here and there did a drunkard stagger out of the open door of a cellar pub, or a solitary cab rattled over the damaged wooden pavement, which lay still widely torn up in places, waiting for its annual holes to be patched up in beautiful mosaic work.

Lost bell sounds, the last from one of the countless churches, quivered over the deserted streets, like the tolling of a bell over a dead city.

Erik walked home slowly, with weary steps.

»Not allowing her to suffer harm,« he repeated the words he had just heard. Yes, that was exactly what he wanted. It was still possible to transplant her into new soil if he carefully replanted his little tree with all its fine roots there. Only in this way could he now perform his gardening services for it, so that the tree would not suffer harm in its development, which was still in tightly and firmly closed buds, – opaque on all sides.

For sometimes, something violent awoke in him, – in the nurturing gardener, the criminal impatience of a boy who assaults the spring and destroys the buds to see if a red or a white blossom sleeps in them.

But he stopped himself from the violent act, he himself pulled Ruth from his hand.

Does a father ruin his child, a man no woman, an artist no work?

And it seemed to him his love for Ruth was all of these.

At home, they had waited for him to eat; when he arrived, it was taken in silence. Klare-Bel's hope that Erik would talk about whom he had visited was not fulfilled.

He knew he had to speak of it now. With her and with Ruth. It was the hardest thing.

That was his thought when he finally stood at the window of his study, looking out into the back garden, where Ruth was walking with Jonas: »Just don't speak, – just don't ponder, – act! Take her in your arms and carry her away. Act! If only one could do it wordlessly!«

And now Jonas went into the house.

Erik descended to Ruth in the garden.

She was sitting in her favorite spot, the stone edge of the fountain. There she sat with her head bowed, poking at the grass with a dry branch.

When she saw him coming, she threw her branch away and ran to him. He had barely greeted her at the late lunch, and now her hand slipped into his.

Without really noticing what he was doing, he put her hand along with his own into the side pocket of his coat.

Ruth laughed at this and looked up at him, but when she saw the serious, almost stern expression on his face, she suddenly fell silent.

They walked a few steps toward the small grove.

»Today I was at your relatives, Ruth,« said Erik, »they were both there. I wanted to ask them something about what we have often discussed together in recent months. Don't you remember? I mean whether you should go abroad to continue your studies properly.«

She looked at him expectantly. This interested her very much, and it also unsettled her a bit. Because it was really just a generally held, vague future picture, – not something that needed to be considered and discussed now.

»Well? And what did they think about it?« Ruth asked tensely when he remained silent.

»– They have no serious objections, Ruth. Nothing serious. So it was Bernhard Römer we thought of for this. There I would know you were well cared for. It would be almost as if I could stay with you myself.«

Her hand, which he still held, grew cold in his.

»Yes, – but – that's still a long way off!« Ruth said very slowly, and then faster and faster, in growing unrest: »It's still a long way off? A very long way off? I shouldn't – leave soon? From here – leave.«

He held her hand tighter and walked towards the benches under the birch trees.

»Come to me,« he said gently, »sit with me here, my darling, and let's talk about it calmly. Very calmly, – do you hear?«

She followed him silently, but her eyes clung to his serious face with a thousand startled, anxious questions.

»You see, child,« Erik continued, »when we thought of your future here during our joint work, it always appeared to you as a desirable, enticing picture. I wanted you to continue developing later, and you wanted it too. I often thought to myself, watching you: some of what I once strove for myself, you might later realize in a different form. But what stood in the distance as a future possibility must come closer until it becomes an irrevocable reality and present. And I want you to come closer to this thought now, my child.«

»– – How close – – is it?« Ruth asked mistrustfully, but no sooner had it escaped her than she tore her hand from his and pressed both hands flat against her ears.

»No!« she murmured indistinctly, »I don't want to know! please, no! please, please, don't continue.«

For a moment, he closed his eyes.

Then he gently took her hands and forced them down.

»It's no use, my child,« he said firmly, »it's no use shutting yourself off from something irrevocable. We will talk about this now. Because the more you still shrink from it, the more urgent, the sooner it must happen.«

Ruth had turned very pale.

A vague dread rose darkly within her. Of something she couldn't grasp, couldn't clearly understand, but which loomed before her – unexpectedly, suddenly, out of nothing, – shadowy, like a giant specter.

»I can't!« she exclaimed. »It can't be this way! I don't want it to be this way. I can't!«

He bent over her and sought her gaze.

»Really not?« he asked quietly; »not even if you know: I want it? Not even if it is I who takes you by the hand, stands you before something difficult, so that you learn to see it coming, without running away?«

She nestled against him and hid her head on his shoulder.

»I'm afraid,« she said, like a child in the dark, »– something terrible is there, – it's been there since yesterday – and it's coming closer, – ever closer, – very close. Like a monster curling around me. – Is it something terrible – –?«

»Not what you feared yesterday,« he said softly, »– only what you yourself wanted yesterday, yourself demanded. Don't you remember what you promised me? You wanted to obey – unconditionally. I was to test you. If I do, Ruth, – do you withdraw your promise?«

»No!« she replied quickly and straightened up. There was no rebellion against that. Only obedience.

»What does the test consist of?« she asked resolutely, »what should I do?«

He didn't answer immediately. He had furrowed his brows, and his teeth dug into his lip as if he were in physical pain.

A few moments they stayed silently together.

A cool breeze wafted through the trees and threw round yellow birch leaves into their laps. The sun struggled to shine through wide white clouds into the garden, and from the bird nests around, a small, full tone occasionally interrupted the silence.

Then Erik answered in a voice that almost sounded rough: »You should prove yourself as brave in a big thing as you once did in a small one. You should do what you once did when you faced the long approach, – approach of something feared. It was then when Jonas brought the snake into the house. It filled you with such fear. Do you remember what remedy your own bravery found against it?«

»No!« she said, puzzled, and looked up, »what was that remedy?«

»You said: ›Then rather right away!‹«

Ruth sprang up abruptly and made a wild gesture towards him, as if to stop him in time.

Then, without a sound, she collapsed before him in the withered August leaves at his feet.

»Ruth!« he murmured anxiously and spread his arms around her, »my child! my darling! do you hear me?«

But she no longer heard. Her head fell back. She had lost consciousness.

Meanwhile, Jonas had run into the garden, who had watched from the window that the father had gone into the small grove with Ruth.

He stood petrified when he now saw Erik emerge from the trees, Ruth limp in his arms, her eyes closed. Her right hand was laid by the father around his neck, the left hung limply.

»Go ahead!« Erik commanded the boy, »without noise. Hold the doors open for me. I must carry Ruth to her bed.«

Jonas's questions stuck in his throat; he ran ahead, not without constantly looking back at the father, and into the house. There, without alarming the mother or Gonne, he ran up the wooden staircase to Ruth's attic room. When Erik arrived with Ruth in his arms, Jonas stood waiting at the wide-open door, through which one could see the narrow white bed with the turned-down cover.

Jonas looked anxiously and pleadingly at his father's face; he would have liked to go in to stay with Ruth. But Erik walked past him silently and closed the door behind him.

This moment imprinted itself on him with remarkable force: how the father, carrying Ruth, passed him so silently while he had to stay behind.

In the father's look and expression, he felt something extraordinary, a rigid, wordless seriousness, – as if Ruth were already as good as dead.

Jonas shuddered.

He clung to the door handle and listened, holding his breath. At first, he distinguished nothing. Then he heard Erik's voice, half aloud, short, very determined in tone. It repeated itself. Then a pause, – and suddenly a wail inside, a single cry, but so painful that the boy was gripped by terror.

What was being done to Ruth, to his dear Ruth? What was the father doing to her? It had to be something terrible. Something terrible must have happened in the small grove today.

And he dared not push open the door, he didn't dare. But a quick, wild feeling, like sudden hatred, flared up in him: that he was a boy, and his father a man! That he couldn't intrude with equal right, – with force!

But just as quickly, it died down again. Ruth could come to no harm if she was with his father.

Jonas crept down to Klare-Bel's small room next to the living room. He couldn't be alone.

There he sat down at the entrance on the edge of a chair and burst into tears.

»Ruth is half dead, Mama!« he said, beside himself, »oh Mama, she's dying! She's already closed her eyes. And Papa, – I don't know what Papa is doing, but he's definitely hurting her. But she can't die! Just now, she was so happy and rustling through the leaves with me in the garden.«

Klare-Bel was no less shocked than he was at this report, and they waited with anxious tension to see if Erik would come down soon. But it was a long time before he came.

»For God's sake, what happened to Ruth?« she called out to him in great distress.

»Just be calm, it was a faint,« Erik replied and gave Jonas a sign to leave. Then he approached his wife and said: »I had to give Ruth news she wasn't sufficiently prepared for. Now you must also know: Ruth is leaving in the coming days. To Heidelberg, to Römer's house.«

Klare-Bel raised herself a little on her pillows and looked at him in deep astonishment.

»Are you serious? You're giving Ruth away? But what will you do without Ruth? Can you do without her?«

»I must be able to, Bel.«

In the growing twilight, she couldn't make out his features clearly. But they seemed to her as if carved from stone. And she knew this expression.

»Erik!« she said anxiously, »don't do anything so violently. You see it makes her ill. – Why do you look so hard, Erik?«

»Hard?« He ran his hand over his forehead; »I can't help my appearance. But don't worry about anything. Ruth will be well and composed tomorrow. I guarantee her composure. But be kind and gentle to her. I have to travel for a day or two.«

»Travel? You're leaving, Erik? Where to?«

»To Moscow.«

»To Mrs. Römer?« she asked eagerly.

»Yes. Ruth is to join her. And she will probably not stay here again. I must therefore arrange everything with her. In person.«

Klare-Bel remained silent. It grew dim in the room, and outside in the hallway, one could hear Jonas pacing restlessly.

Then, very softly, Erik felt his hand being taken by Klare-Bel.

»Erik!« she whispered, »– let me ask you: let her stay with us a little longer. – – – I will miss her too, Erik!«

»You – – – Bel?«

»Yes. Because she made you so happy.«

He drew her hand to himself and to his mouth and kissed it full of shame and reverence.

»I thank you for this request. I thank you, Bel. But it can't be.«

He withdrew to inform Ruth's uncle of the final decision. Then he packed a handbag, and an hour later, he was gone. He still traveled on the night train to Moscow.

In that night, Klare-Bel lay awake for a long time, thinking of Ruth and Erik. She had firmly believed that Ruth would stay with them in the house until late autumn and then, even in her uncle's house, remain closely connected with them. How often had they joked about whether she should go to university later with Jonas? Erik had not said a word that his intentions might have been different from the start. Now, he suddenly revealed them.

But Klare-Bel certainly did not think of criticizing this way of acting. Since he wanted it this way, it must be good. Good for Ruth. He loved her so much; he could only have her best interest in mind. Even though it came upon them so unexpectedly.

But she would have liked to go up to Ruth now and comfort and console her. She resolved to do it the next day. For the first time, she felt a truly motherly affection for Ruth—not just the indirect interest that went through Erik and related everything to him.

The morning was autumnal and gray, the terrace still damp from the cold mists of the night. They had to have breakfast in the living room. Ruth appeared at the usual time; she was pale and serious but healthy, as Erik had said, and quite composed and quiet.

When she came in, even before Jonas, Klare-Bel stretched out her arms to her: "Come to me," she said lovingly, "don't be sad, don't think about the departure. You're still here!"

Ruth looked up without changing her calm expression and shook her head.

"I am already gone!" she replied.

This answer deeply moved Klare-Bel. It seemed to her that there was something more painful in it than in complaints and tears—something that already felt the mere announcement of the separation as a complete separation and could not let go of it.

She felt a surge of hot compassion within her. And now Erik seemed hard to her. How could he want Ruth to go from house to house, from hand to hand? Unconsciously, she searched for words that could truly comfort. Were there none? In her helplessness, she reached for the highest thing she knew.

"We never know where we will stay or what will happen to us," she said hesitantly, "we never know. It is in God's hands. But we are also never alone, wherever we go. God is omnipresent."

Ruth smiled fleetingly.

"Yes," she said sadly, "what good does it do that God is omnipresent when people, the people we leave, are not?"

Klare-Bel was painfully silent. She gave up trying to comfort Ruth. When she said something like that, it sounded childish and presumptuous at the same time. Who could respond to that?

Ruth did not mention Erik's absence; although he had not spoken to her about it, she was not surprised not to see him. It had to be this way: everything was falling apart.

Jonas knew nothing of the impending separation. No one told him. He only heard that Ruth was healthy again, but he didn't believe it. How could she be healthy when she was so completely changed since yesterday? And not only Ruth, everything seemed changed to him.

He would have liked to ask her to tell him what happened yesterday, but she walked past him all day with such an inward, distant look that he couldn't bring himself to ask. So he contented himself with sitting next to her as often as he could, his arm around her chair, and occasionally stroking her hand gently and tenderly. Sometimes he would bend down and kiss her hand without Ruth noticing.

Erik's absence heightened Jonas's feeling that he had to watch over Ruth like a faithful guardian. He would have liked to defend her with body and soul and save her from mortal danger—if only he knew from what and from whom.

Late in the evening, when she had long since gone up to her little room, Jonas still patrolled tirelessly in the garden in front of her window, regretting that nothing was happening. Finally, he went to bed with a convulsive yawn but slept restlessly and soon woke up again.

Then he clearly saw Ruth's window cross silhouetted against a bright patch of light in the garden: there must still be light burning in her room at dawn.

Was she sick? Unhappy?

He couldn't stay in bed. In a moment, he was dressed and climbed silently out of the window. In front of the terrace stood the old elm; it formed a comfortable saddle where it forked into two mighty branches. Like a cat, Jonas climbed the mossy trunk, made slippery by the heavy dew during the night.

He longingly looked into the yellowish candlelight that fell from the attic room.

Ruth was sitting on the bed. Fully dressed, as she had gone up, she was still sitting there; her arms stretched out in front of her, her hands folded on her knees, almost turning her face towards Jonas. Her head slightly raised, she looked far over the dark treetops of the garden.

She looked so mysterious, as if into an infinite, transfigured distance. And around her tightly closed lips lay a calm expression—resignation.

Jonas stared at her with wide-open eyes. He was so captivated by the one image that he did not consciously perceive what the flickering light on the table illuminated. He did not see that the table was cleared, the chairs pushed together—that on them stood an open, half-filled suitcase and that the walls, without the decoration of his pencil sketches, looked bare and empty at Ruth.

He only saw her, his cheerful Ruth, as in the image of a praying saint, and everything that had stirred his heavy boyish imagination in the previous day's events gained renewed power over him. Ruth herself became something mysterious and suffering to him, transforming from the joyful playmate into a being that awakened his reverie.

In his mind, he heard again the soft lament from the previous day, he saw her lying on the bed, the father bent over her—and his heart beat anxiously.

He couldn't take his eyes off the window.

The night was cold, the mist rising from the lawn beneath him. Narrow and pale, the small crescent moon hung in the eastern sky, and from the woods came the sleepy cawing of a raven.

Jonas shivered, he pushed his hands under his thin summer jacket and pressed himself closer to the broad branches, whose dampness gradually soaked him. In doing so, one of his red slippers fell with a splash onto the terrace below.

He pulled the bare foot under him and considered irritably whether to climb down to retrieve the lost shoe. Then Ruth moved. The noise outside had awakened her from her dreamlike state.

She stood up slowly and took off her blouse.

An arm emerged, and beneath the shirt not covered by a corset, the delicate curve of her breast.

For a moment she stood still with her head bowed. Then she raised her bare arms high above her, fell to her knees before her bed, and threw herself over it with outstretched arms, her upper body stretched out, buried in the pillows. She remained motionless.

Jonas remained unmoving and held his breath. He had forgotten the shoe, he had forgotten the cold.

His eyes flickered.

Bent far forward, his fingers clawed into the leafy branches to keep from falling, he stared with pounding temples at the bed.

The morning dawned slowly above him.

-

When Gonne picked up the slipper while sweeping the terrace early in the morning, Jonas had long since limped back to his bed, shivering from cold and excitement, half-unconscious. He made a great effort the next day to hide a severe indisposition, but he could barely speak due to hoarseness, and his eyes shone with fever. When Klare-Bel anxiously pressed and questioned him, he confessed to having sat in the garden the whole night.

After lunch, he threw himself on his bed fully dressed.

Around this time, Erik returned home. Klare-Bel had expected him only at nightfall. But he had also taken the night train from Moscow.

Ruth was in his study, trying to sort out her papers and notebooks from his to pack them. What was his and what was hers? The entire content of her studies in notes written by his hand, the entire content of his plans and work for the winter, his thoughts and lectures transcribed, written down by her hand.

Then she unexpectedly heard a quick, firm step in the hallway.

The door to Erik's room flew open, and Ruth ran into his arms.

She had not thought about the purpose and duration of his trip. Hypnotized by the single certainty that she had to leave, she accepted everything passively.

But the sudden sight of Erik now had a powerful effect on her. In this one moment, she forgot everything—in this one moment, the power of the present overcame every sorrow that lay ahead—denied it, annihilated it—in this moment, everything became good.

She could think of nothing but that he was there. And that she was with him.

Firmly, firmly, her arms wrapped around his neck, her face nestled against his shoulder.

To remain standing like this, to remain standing like this forever, rooted forever in this spot, nestled into the wide, soft folds of the open traveling cloak—to feel nothing, to perceive nothing but the strong, muffled heartbeat that pounded against her—for her whole life, nothing more.

They exchanged no words.

Erik's travel bag slipped from his hand to the floor; silently he held Ruth to his chest, breathing heavily, his head bowed over her hair.

And suddenly his hands dug hard into her shoulders, around her hips, enclosing her with such a violent grip that it felt like pain and suffocation to her, as if he had to break her now. Break under his hands and against his chest—she thought, and it flooded her with a jubilant feeling of happiness she had never known.

Erik saw her smile.

He lost his senses.

"Madness!" it shot through his head like fire, "Madness! Madness to let go when you love each other."

For a second—then he let her go so abruptly that she staggered back—

And: "Erik!" Klare-Bel's voice called through the next room, "Erik, are you back?"

He hung his coat on the stand, then opened the door to the living room where she lay.

"Just think, Erik, Jonas has fallen ill in the meantime—such a severe cold—I hope it's not too bad. He has—but what's wrong with you?"

He stood there like a stunned man, bloodshot eyes.

"Nothing. A dizziness," he muttered, sat down at the table, and rested his head on his hands.

"It's this exaggerated haste!" she lamented worriedly, "—that it all has to happen with such whirlwind speed. When exactly is it that she is leaving, Erik?"

"Tomorrow—around noon," he said softly.

"My God, so quickly, but that is simply impossible! Just think of all the things that need to be arranged and considered for such a departure. Ruth surely still needs many things that have to be procured."

"Everything can be procured in Heidelberg."

"Well, Erik. But if you knew how deeply it affects her. How pale and miserable she looked, yesterday and today. She is so delicate."

"Stop!" he said through clenched teeth.

"Oh, Erik, I'm not contradicting you! I never do! She just makes me so sad. So alone she is, and so in need of love. And now: from house to house, from hand to hand. And if she falls ill—"

"Stop!" he interrupted her, beside himself, sprang up, and threw the chair back so that it crashed to the floor, "stop, Bel! It's enough! I want it this way!"

With that, he left the room.

She looked after him with startled eyes. Erik was almost always gentle with her, even though—or perhaps because—her will never really came into consideration against his. She had not seen him in such a violent outburst for a long time—not since her sickbed. The sick are good teachers!

Only in the first years of their marriage. Then his quick temper had not yet faded, then he became easily angry if his wife did not fully correspond to what he had expected, what he had wanted with her.

Strangely, it did not frighten her then—no, more so, as odd as it might be: she loved this anger. So clearly she felt that Erik's love was linked with it. He could never be angry with someone indifferent to him. With his interest in a person grew in this imperious nature the desire to shape, to form, to reshape them according to his will. Love and hardness fell together.

Klare-Bel had seen a Russian storybook, on the cover of which were two peasant women: one, in a red sarafan, being beaten by her husband with a willow stick, laughing across her face; the second, in a blue sarafan, sitting on a stone by the roadside, crying her eyes out, while her husband walked with another woman.

It was surely a silly story. But Klare-Bel could well understand these two peasant women.

She would never be frightened by his anger: only that he should not forget his love in his anger.

The day crept slowly to an end. It was as quiet in the house as if no one were there. Erik had sat with Jonas for a long time, looked at him closely, arranged everything necessary, and forced the fiercely resisting boy to stay in bed. It was a severe throat infection with considerable fever.

Ruth stood in the hallway, leaning against the banister. She herself did not know why she stood there. Probably because all the doors opened into the hallway. And from one of the doors, Erik had to finally come. And when he came, he had to come to her. Turn to her. He had to realize that it was impossible to pass by each other so distantly, as he did this evening.

She wanted so little: only to see his gaze directed at her—only to feel his hand for a moment.

Since Erik had torn her to himself and then pushed her away, a helpless despair had come over her. She accepted the external separation, as something terrible but unavoidable because he demanded it. But the fact that he suddenly tore her away from him internally as well, she could not bear. To see him deliberately avert his eyes—without a word of love for her, to see him standing like a stranger—that she certainly could not bear.

At bedtime, Erik stepped out of the living room. When he noticed Ruth on the stairs, he wished her good night. She made a movement towards him, her eyes looking up at him darkly and reproachfully. But he did not look into her eyes. He only gave her hand a fleeting touch. Then he passed by her into Jonas's room.

Soon after, exhaustion overcame him; unexpectedly, he fell into a heavy slumber. But disturbing and ugly dreams filled his sleep, terrible dreams that covered his body with cold sweat.

He saw Ruth before him, aged, withered, with furrowed features and pinched lips, with lips given by an empty, loveless youth; he saw her in a ridiculous image, like in a farce as a virtuous hysterical old maid, with unfulfilled longing for affection in her extinct gaze. And then, as he forced his eyes away from the apparition in the dream, away to another image of Ruth—then it transformed before him—into naked, exposed beauty. Naked he saw Ruth—and shameless, offered to strange men—a white body that was not hers, a laughing face that was not hers—and yet he knew: it was Ruth.

He woke with a groaning sound. And even from the dream, he heard kissing and laughing.

But the faint moaning repeated itself, as if it had found an echo on the walls of the room, and a suppressed crying reached Erik's ear.

He sat up and listened.

The crying came from Jonas's bed, which stood beside the open connecting door of the two rooms. One could clearly hear him trying to stifle it in the pillows.

Erik fully awakened. He made light and approached Jonas's bed. When Jonas heard him coming, he burrowed deeper into his covers.

"Do you have pain?" he heard his father ask, "are you feeling worse?"

"I'm not sick!" Jonas muttered, "it's pointless to keep me in bed by force. I know everything! I know everything now! It was no use hiding it from me! And what I didn't know, I heard! I listened and heard it!"

Erik was silent for a moment, taken aback. "You are speaking in a fever," he said then; "what do you know, what did you hear?"

"That she is leaving! That she is leaving tomorrow!" And he buried himself sobbing into his pillows.

Erik reached for his face and placed his hand worriedly on his dry, burning forehead. But Jonas pushed the hand away.

"No," he said, almost panting, "you want it—you are the reason she is leaving. I have to protect Ruth from you—protect her because you don't know—how she feels. You don't know, you haven't seen—how she lies awake at night—half-undressed on her bed—like yesterday."

Erik squeezed the fever-glowing hand in his, so that Jonas clenched his teeth to control the pain.

"What did you—see yesterday?" Erik asked in a hoarse voice.

Jonas sat up.

"She knelt before her bed," he said sadly, "maybe she was crying—or praying—her eyes were so mysterious—and I watched over her—the whole night, secretly, up in the old elm in front of the terrace."

Erik did not speak a word.

But after a long pause, he raised his hand, and gently stroked Jonas's forehead and hair. This time the hand was not pushed away. The gentle, caressing movement of the father, who so rarely caressed him, felt to Jonas like a wordless understanding and empathy that brought him to the brink of losing control.

And suddenly he threw his arms around his father's neck. And like an unstoppable stream, feverishly hot, half-incomprehensible words broke out of him, tumbled over each other, and faded into stammering: "Papa, dear Papa, help me! I can't stand it that she is leaving! I was angry with you—don't hold it against me—help me! Keep her here! Papa! She will stay if you only want it. I used to be jealous of Ruth, I thought you loved her more than me. But it doesn't matter how much you love her, Papa! Because I love her so much more than you! More than you! More than anything in the world!"

Erik quietly loosened the hands from his neck and held them firmly.

"Compose yourself," he said in a low voice, but with the insistent tone Jonas was absolutely used to following, "you cannot lie here and lose control like this. Not even in a fever. Compose yourself."

Almost mechanically, Jonas tried to obey. He breathed heavily.

Erik had sat on the edge of the bed without letting go of his hands.

"Lie down. Completely still. Suppress the agitation. Come, my boy! More firmly! And now listen to me: I will help you if you follow me, but differently than you think. You must part from Ruth now. We all must. For she is leaving tomorrow, and until then you will not be allowed to get up."

Jonas sprang up.

"Papa! I must! I will jump out of bed! You won't stop me! I must kiss Ruth—I must kiss her—when she leaves!"

"With a sore, inflamed throat and fever, you will not want to kiss Ruth, I hope," Erik interrupted him in a tone that brooked no argument, "and you will not only refrain from it but also do everything I ask of you. You will completely control yourself when she bids you farewell. With no words, no outburst, not a single complaining sound, you will make it harder for her. Suppress all excitement with firm will. You will do all this. I must be able to rely on you completely if I am to bring her to you. Can I?"

"Yes!" Jonas choked out, his lips still trembling. He could not resist this will that held his own in thrall.

"Good. And now I will give you a comforting solace for your first great sorrow," said Erik in such a soft voice that it seemed to Jonas as if he were speaking to him in the tones of his mother.

"When Ruth has left you, do not look back at her, but forward into your life; ensure that you develop strongly, work to become a whole man soon—so that you can be a true friend to her when she needs you. In everything you do, come back to her—be near her. Do not allow her to completely outdistance you and leave you far behind! Now you can show what you are worth—and whether you were worthy of having Ruth."

Jonas lay completely still and listened.

"Yes!" he said enthusiastically, "I will! Oh, Papa, I will!"

And he lifted his head and kissed his father. Erik held his head to him for a moment.

"We will never speak of this again," he said quietly, "never again. But do not forget. Direct your thoughts to work, to what lies ahead of you. Learn to control yourself more firmly. I will watch over you and let nothing slip. Be strict with yourself, my boy. Do not make it too hard for me."

"Papa," Jonas replied as trustingly as he only ever spoke to Klare-Bel, "I will never fear you again. Be as strict as you want with me. You are helping me, aren't you? To become strong. As strong and capable as no other. I must outdo everyone else! Help me quickly to become a whole man!—A man for—for—I mean: a friend for Ruth."

He would have liked to sit up in bed and chatter; Erik had to forbid him to talk and leave the room. Now he lay silently and contentedly in bed, thinking intensely about the future.

Erik was unable to go back to sleep; he dressed completely. He felt refreshed, as if from a long, healthy sleep, as if cooled and steeled by a refreshing bath. The oppressive malaise of the afternoon and evening, which had weighed on his dreams, had vanished. In influencing another, whose unrest he subdued, whose innermost, resistant thoughts he directed—in the brief struggle with the boy who rebelled against him and yet trusted him, he had found himself again. Awakened and gathered his strength. He knew very well how it stood: when he felt weakest, he grew stronger by the art of making others strong through superior handling; in the uplifted and courageous mood he demanded from them and aroused in them—in his own convinced, persuasive words, he climbed to new courage, new confidence, as if on a long ladder that rose from his own despondency but seemed to reach into the infinite—into an unlimited self-confidence.

Many thousands of such ladders, held by the hands of a crowd of people who surrounded him, believed in him, relied on him—and he would have ascended to a heaven on earth.

Just no collapsing of the firmest of these supports! for supports they were—however much he appeared as the supporter himself. No one is absolutely strong.

Erik knew very well where his danger lay, where the weakling also lurked within him: there, where he was left to himself alone.

Outside, it was still dark night. It struck three o'clock.

He couldn't bear being in the narrow, warm room. He quietly opened the front door and stepped out.

The darkness was so dense that he could only slowly proceed towards the depths of the garden. He sensed the rising mist without seeing it. The rustling of the birch treetops informed him of the proximity of the small grove. Above it, a lost star shone here and there in the veiled sky. The last quarter of the moon, the pale precursor of the dawn, was not yet visible.

Not far from the benches at the grove, Erik stopped to listen. He heard absolutely nothing but the gentle rustling of the leaves. But he felt that he was not alone.

"Ruth!" he murmured involuntarily.

"Yes! What should I do?" she asked timidly.

With one step he was beside the bench, he reached out for her.

"What you should do?! Be in bed!"

He tore his jacket from his shoulders and threw it around her.

"What are you doing here in the middle of the night? Don't you know that Jonas caught the fever in this dangerous cold dampness?"

"Yes, I know. But it doesn't harm me," she replied hesitantly, "the fever feels so good, I know it well: there one lies in a dream and stops thinking. And I thought I could have it as well."

Now she felt his hand, which firmly grasped her wrist.

"What are you saying?" he asked very slowly, "you sought the fever?"

"No, no!" she cried pleadingly, "I only wanted it a little—a very little only—not enough to delay the departure! Certainly not!"

A sound escaped his lips as if he were wounded. She could hear his teeth softly grinding against each other.

He leaned over her.

"And that—that you thought you could do," he said weakly.

"Yes, I could, for I am doing what I promised. I am not disobedient. But I am so alone. No one to help me a little. So the fever should help me. I can do what I want—as long as it doesn't delay anything," she replied darkly.

"I see. And if you just leave in time, then you think—you can do what you want? Also perhaps sit down somewhere and get sick if that 'helps' you? You are mistaken, my child. I am not letting you go by letting you leave. And from afar, you must obey me doubly. Your promise extends over your whole life. You are mine. Are you?"

"Yes!" she cried fervently.

"Get up and go upstairs."

"I can't do it like this—I must first know—when am I leaving?"

"I will tell you tomorrow. Not tonight. You are to lie down and try to sleep. Think of nothing but that you are to sleep. Will you?"

She was already standing up.

"Yes," she murmured, "tomorrow! I must ask tomorrow what I want."

"You shall."

He gave her his hand.

"Go ahead. Just go. I will follow. Do not wait for me in the house."

"Good night!" she said obediently and went. "My darling! good night!" he called after her. And in the tone of his voice lay all the endearments she had longed for all day, all night.

"Forgive me! Darling," he said contritely to himself as he slowly followed her. He had left her alone, left her standing alone at the moment when she expected and needed all his strength and love. Because he did not trust himself, did not trust himself—out of fear of his senses—and this innocent child's sense, which smiled at him.

That had been cowardly. He should not withdraw his hand in the last hour for such cowardly reasons, the hand she reached for longingly and trustingly, as for the hand of the only person the earth carried for her. Not calculate, not withhold, not limit what he gave her, and what she longed for with an intensity—as tenderly as only the lonely, never caressed child knows.

Out of an infinite abundance, his love should envelop her once more, surround her, soft and protective like motherly love—from such a rich, secure abundance that he could rid himself of all doubts—that he lifted and carried his dearest, carrying her like a sleeping child in a last dream over into the foreign, colder world.

The hallway was dimly lit by the light from Erik's room. Ruth hung his jacket over the doorknob, and without looking back at Erik, she went upstairs.

He extinguished the flickering, dripping light in the draft and stretched out on the leather couch in his study, glad of the darkness and solitude.

Since the moment of his return yesterday, he had unconsciously longed for this quiet and solitude.

At the moment when he stepped into his wife's room from the hallway yesterday, at the moment when Ruth lay in his arms and Bel's voice called him, something strange had happened inside him. She called: "Erik, are you back?"—But it pierced him like: "Erik, are you leaving me?" And when he saw her again, saw her lying there in the room he knew so well, just as two days ago, it seemed to him as if a long, long—years-long journey lay between, during which he had not seen his wife, had not taken her with him—yes, forgotten her. It had been almost like a moment of mental derangement.

And the excitement, in which all his nerves still trembled, allowed no self-reflection.

But now—now he stood back in that place, opposite Bel and her questioning voice, and now he answered her: "It has been a long, long journey. I have not seen you all this time—there where you are: forgotten you.

Not accidentally, not unintentionally, not in the intoxication of the moment. No, consciously and deliberately. With all my senses and thoughts, I wanted to have only one point before my eyes, to see through it, to penetrate—to look into a veiled future. Unhindered by everything that hinders and binds. Free, like one who has thrown everything behind and stands like a beggar or a king, I wanted to lift my hands to my happiness.

Then—once—it is time to return to the questions and demands, the duties and bonds of daily life, but only to deal with them. To return to you, but only for the fight. The fight for my happiness."

Erik had almost murmured the last words aloud: "Fight—happiness."

He opened his eyes as if waking.

It was bright around him. The night was over. The sky stood glowing red, as if in flames.

Behind the grove, the sun was rising. Purplish, without rays, like a huge moon, it shone through the morning mist. And purplish light on the windows, on the floor.

No one in the house could yet be heard. Only the blackbirds chattered near the kitchen window, wondering if Gonne would soon throw them some crumbs while preparing the first breakfast?

Erik stood still, facing the splendor of the morning.

He had loved Bel—as much as, in his opinion so far, a man could love a woman: not only with the greed of the senses, not only for a fleeting love union that happened to be called "marriage," but for a real life union that no state, no priest, only his own conscious will could seal. It had been as he once said in a joking conversation about marriage to Warwara: not just a sense of duty but the constant awareness of the happiness of being everything to his wife, even after the sensual love had faded. Neither sickbeds nor aging, neither life's disappointments nor temptations of love had ever been able to change the slightest thing.

If he had ever been unfaithful to her in a passionate outburst of lust—or even in a bitter reflection on the shattered, given-up hopes of his youth—he had fought against it with strength and hardness against himself. He would never admit that any power could be stronger over him than his will, his surety.

And now, if he gathered all he had of shame and self-confidence, of pride and heart's kindness—if he gathered and bundled it all, was it not enough to protect Bel, the defenseless, against a struggle with him? Or if in the future such a struggle arose, was there nothing in his past life strong enough, holy enough, merciful enough to intervene for Bel and triumph against himself?

Erik looked straight ahead, into the red sea of flames in the sky. He wanted—he had to be honest.

And he said to himself: "No."

•

On the terrace, the breakfast table was being set. But today, Erik's place at the table remained empty. Early in the morning, he had ordered tea to his room, then he had gone to see Jonas.

Immediately after breakfast, he had Ruth sent to him.

When she came, he stretched out his hand to her. "You bad girl. Have you stayed healthy? Let me see."

She nodded and stepped up to him at the old leather armchair by the window.

He examined her closely. Her eyes were darkly shadowed. But they looked steady—firm. It struck him. They looked almost cold.

He brushed her hair back from her pale face.

"Do you still know that this is your old place? Here by the chair. Where you first came. We have almost forgotten it, outside in the garden and—with the others. For months. But this morning belongs to us alone. To us both. And you wanted to spend it sick."

She did not answer.

She only gently bent her head towards him, so that his hand slid through the waves of her hair, and remained silent.

"You are a silly child," he said, "otherwise you would have known: when I ask something of you, you are to do it clearly and quietly. Never in a feverish frenzy. In no sense. I know, it is a thousand times harder. But you must never make it easier for yourself. Not in any way. Only I myself was not without fault this time, Ruth. I myself was like sick—not as I should be.

You see, now I am confessing to you too.—Is it good now?"

She looked at him intently. Then she shook her head.

"One thing is still missing," she said.

A smile came to him.

"Something more? What then, my demanding little head?"

"May I not be demanding?"

"You may. Hold your hands open, darling, and let yourself be given to."

Then she slid down by the armchair to her old place at his knees and raised her face to him—defiance in her eyes.

"I don't mean a gift. A right." Erik paused.

He looked searchingly into her eyes, with the firm, enigmatic gaze directed at him.

"Take your right, Ruth," he said simply.

She whispered, barely audible: "To know why. The sudden having to leave—why?"

He placed his hand over her eyes.

A long pause ensued.

"You were right earlier: one thing is missing," he replied then, "between us one thing is missing. Do you know what it is? That between you and me lies too great a span of human life—that we are so far apart in age. Think: you and you again, that still does not give: me. At such a great distance, it is sometimes difficult to share some things—to communicate. But now see the wonder: this lack, this gap and emptiness between you and me—they unite us. Only they make it so that I can guide you and command you. They make it so that you can kneel there so trustfully, as just now, and look up to me with your defiant eyes. They make it so that I know the way better than you. Because I have already traveled half the way. Or could you do without that? Would you prefer I stood beside you, of the same height as you? Still searching, erring, needing a guide, like you?"

"No!" she said eagerly, "that would be like two children in the woods."

"Then accept that I do not answer you."

She said nothing, but he felt her heart begin to beat wildly. She did not passively yield as she had until yesterday. Yesterday she had grown confused with him.

With the last of her strength, she might have gathered herself against him, convinced herself that she still had strength: independence. Shaken in innocent sleep, her feelings might have come to ferment—a world of uncomprehended emotions struggling within her.

The fine, calm, straight line in which she had developed so childishly before Erik's eyes became indistinct, became restless—it seemed to bend—to make a turn: a turn towards him—or away from him.

A tension came over Erik that sharpened all his mental faculties to the utmost, tensed his whole being in anticipation, and completely suppressed any sensual excitement.

He put his arm around Ruth and bent her head back with his hand. Her lips quivered.

"Look me in the eyes, you defiant child!" he said, "what has stirred in you? Break the last defiance—because it was one. Let me break it. It doesn't hurt if it hurts for a moment. Yield, let it happen. Throw your right away, make yourself truly free. To have the right of a child: to obey without asking. To go without a why."

"When—to go?" she asked indistinctly.

He pressed her head to him.

"Today," he said with a covered voice, "now. Right now. No, do not start. Be my brave child. We only have this hour, Ruth. Then I will take you to town. To the train that goes abroad. Mrs. Römer is waiting for us."

She had thrown herself into his arms. She embraced him as if nothing could tear her away from there. Yet he knew: she no longer resisted. She yielded, without will.

But it might only be the fear of parting. The shock of it that overwhelmed her. Yesterday she had become confused with him—and tomorrow?—then he would have no power over her anymore. He would no longer know what was going on inside her.

He said very gently: "You are not going because I want to hurt you, but because I love you. So much that I can hurt you. Give yourself to this love, Ruth—without reserve, without doubt—give yourself to it completely. Be grateful every day that I say to you—in the morning when you wake, in the evening when you sleep: 'I love you.'"

She looked up, still holding onto him—with boundless gratitude in her eyes she looked up. A faint smile played around her mouth—a little hesitant still.

"Then I am not leaving—then I am taking you with me," she said, almost impishly.

Happiness broke from her eyes—yes, the prankster.

It intoxicated him. But differently than yesterday. While he held her in his arms, while she knelt at his chest, it was not his senses that were intoxicated. Something infinitely finer, a pleasure so fine that it could not be mediated through any senses, filled him with powerful satisfaction. He could not more completely take possession of Ruth, make her more his own, than in this moment when he released her, when she left at his command because he loved her.

Union and separation, selfless renunciation and selfish intervention, protection and violence, service and domination intertwined indistinguishably in a single knot of feelings, in a single moment of intoxicating experience.

"Isn't it good now that you must obey and trust me? That we are not like 'two children in the woods' who get lost? For whom it would be bad if one lost sight of the other—left. You disappear from my sight, but never from my hand. I am with you like someone you do not see standing next to you, yet know around you—ruling over you wherever you go and stand. Like someone you cannot ask, and who remains silent about many things—yet knows everything that you need and is good for you like—"

"Like God," Ruth said boldly.

The word ran like a shudder over him. Out of ghostly fear?

No. But surely because he sensed what might awaken in her with this word, of unconscious, immense demanding and admiration and expectation.

She did not say it in ecstasy. Like something self-evident. Like a child gives a kiss.

But he sensed: never, never before had she been so close to love, to full love, as in this childlike confession—the most presumptuous.

No, no ghostly fear! of nothing. And he kissed her hair.

"Not like God, Ruth. And yet let it be for you: like your God."

•

In the living room, Klare-Bel was busy closing Ruth's suitcase and filling her a small travel bag. Gonne helped to arrange and procure the last things. Outside at the garden gate stood a light cart, a rural "karfaschka," which was to take the luggage. Erik wanted to walk to the station with Ruth.

When the luggage was loaded, he came out with her from his study. Klare-Bel looked almost incredulously. Neither he nor Ruth had sad faces. And yet she knew: only now had he told Ruth there in the room.

"How does he manage to do it? He can do whatever he wants!" she thought admiringly.

The little cart rattled off, constantly in danger of losing one of its wobbly wheels on the bumpy country road. Erik joked about it, and Ruth had her dimpled cheeks in her face.

It was a cheerfulness as if a ray of sun sparkled on the surface of a great silent, dark water, covering it with glittering pearls.

Only Gonne stood in the kitchen and cried with a surly, embarrassed face.

For a few more minutes, Ruth was able to stay in Jonas's room. Then she came out ready for travel, the gray woolen cap on her head.

Jonas listened intently. He heard her walking across the hall—the last greeting call from his mother—the doors opened—then a minute's pause—and now the garden gate creaked shut with a faint sound.

•

Slowly, silently, the hours crept by, one after the other. Early in the afternoon, Erik returned from town.

But it remained as quiet as before.

Jonas could no longer stay in bed; he got up, with his wet wrap around his neck, a thick woolen stocking tied over it, he stole into his father's study on his red slippers.

The father was not there.

Jonas sat at the big desk. He had to finish before his father surprised him here.

And his pen scratched across the paper. He wrote to Ruth:

"Sweet, dear Ruth!

I have sat at Papa's desk where you worked.

How terribly much I would have liked to go to the station! But I didn't want to cry, I bit into the pillow. But when the train whistled far away (perhaps it wasn't even your train), I cried a little anyway. I thought: now she's leaving.

But Papa gave me good advice. I won't tell you what kind yet. I'd rather follow it first. And as long as I have to follow it, which may take a long time, I won't write to you. But then I will write to you that you must become my wife. In play you never wanted to, and that hurt me sometimes so much. But that was silly of me. Because first, I must become a whole man for you.

I didn't dare to say anything about it to Papa yet.

Now I must finish. But I had to write it to you right away, so you know. Just don't forget me if you find another boy there. In the end, even a finished student? Then all my efforts here would be in vain.

But maybe you won't find one.

I kiss you with a thousand kisses.

Your friend

(Your future husband) Jonas.

P.S.: I don't know where Papa is now, I am up secretly. Otherwise, he would certainly send his regards to you.

Erik was upstairs in the empty little attic room.

He stood at the window and wept.

V.

Like a fledgling bird, fearful Of where it might find refuge, Thus, fleeing, I arrived, A poor child, into your hands.

I seemed to come with defiance, – But driven only by loneliness, And knelt silently by your side, Desiring nothing but to love something.

And wanted nothing but for a short time To feel like a child again, Nothing but a bit of tenderness, Timidly, from afar, to share.

Nothing but to rest for a moment From a deeply childlike torment, Nothing but to unburden A child's heart in fervent devotion.

How well I felt when I found you, As if every wish must be fulfilled, Since you, with gentle hand, Had wholly sheltered me within your will.

As if suddenly everything became clear, As if all confusion must vanish, Since over my disheveled hair Your dear hands stroked.

Until every pain henceforth Sank before magical comfort, Since with the first word of love Your gaze compelled and caressed me;

Until the whole world sank away And nothing of it remained, But only boundless gratitude And only boundless love.

Ruth did not write this. Erik wrote it. But Ruth stammered it. Countless times. Perhaps also in countless verses.

He didn't know. But up in the attic room, amid discarded papers and withered flowers, lay the torn page with the stammered verses.

And since then, he composed these verses, looking ahead and working on them.

Ruth did not write them. Erik did.

But so, – so she would have written them in every word – a little later – in retrospect.

They all sat together.

Klare-Bel in the background of the living room in a large, comfortable armchair. Jonas at the dining table; he had moved the lamp close to better see what he was writing in his school notebook. Erik by the fireplace, where mighty logs were burning; from time to time he bent down and threw a few brown, resinous pinecones from a polished coal bin filled with them into the flames.

The room had taken on a completely wintery look. Instead of the light summer curtains, there were heavy protective window drapes, two armchairs from the city apartment by the fireplace, under which a large bear stretched out its paws.

Already at the beginning of the Russian March, even before winter ended, the move had taken place this year. Because of Klare-Bel. Behind her lay a half-year's path of suffering, slowly leading her to recovery.

In the corner leaned two strong sticks with crutch handles. She had to take a few steps with these sticks every day. "Learning to walk," as Jonas laughingly said, who would have preferred to replace the sticks for her. And these steps she was supposed to take in the fresh air.

They sat together and were silent together. Klare-Bel sat in a half-lying position, pondering; the needlework she had intended slipped from her hands. She felt tired from her few steps.

Jonas was engrossed in his work. With narrow shoulders, grown tall, a little soft blond fuzz on his chin and lip, he bent over his books. For safety, he also had a finger stuck in each ear. That was unnecessary.

And Erik looked into the flames – –

"Until the whole world sank away –"

It was Gonne who finally broke the silence. She brought in the evening tea. Klare-Bel moved behind the samovar: her daily renewed joy of at least being the housewife in such small things again.

"Today you must have been happy, Erik, such a long letter from Ruth," she remarked, "one must say: she writes faithfully, – regularly. Sometimes a note, sometimes a book!"

"I wonder why you've never written to her, Jonas?" asked the father. "She often wants to hear about you."

Jonas turned very red.

"What should one write about? I have enough to do," he mumbled over his teacup.

"For such young people, letter writing is also nothing," Klare-Bel opined, "Ruth is not untalented, is she? And aren't her letters quite dreadfully dry, Erik?"

"Well, yes. When she doesn't have something to tell or describe."

"Describe? What? How a mountain looks, or what the weather is like, – a snowstorm in winter, can't she write pages about that? But I find that one learns very little about her herself."

Erik remained silent. He thought so too. This delight in describing even the slightest thing, the devotion to reproducing what surrounded her and what she immediately absorbed, – all this lay alongside a sparingness of words when it came to her feelings. It wasn't reticence, – it was a hatred of the word, the inadequate one. Scribbling bad verses, singing, stammering, lifting her eyes, – until he had seen that again, heard it again, Ruth was as if buried for him.

And again they were silent.

The tea table was cleared. Only a bowl of apples remained. Jonas made as if to spread out his books and notebooks again.

Erik stopped him.

"Enough!" he said, "it is quite impossible that you should not be finished with your schoolwork yet."

"I am, Papa. But I wanted to study Russian in the evenings now. One of the boys helps me with it during the free period."

"I don't see the point. In the autumn, you'll go abroad. You won't be studying here. So why?"

"It is very useful, Papa. In Germany, one can now earn money with Russian lessons."

Erik was unpleasantly surprised. "Money? By giving lessons? Leave that to me."

"Please allow me. Am I not doing enough for school?"

"Yes, but you have become a terrible homebody, Jonas! You remain too narrow-chested for me, my boy. Down on the chin but no strength in the bones. Not enough."

"Health is not the highest good," Jonas asserted with a seriousness that seemed rather funny.

"But the greatest evil is the guilt of having forfeited it," Erik added, stroking his head affectionately; "if you keep quoting like that, I might take you away from those wretched books altogether. Send you to a farmer for apprenticeship."

With that, he went into his study.

A pile of school notebooks with blue covers was already ready. Also, various other things that were pressing.

He was not pressed. He pushed them aside.

Underneath lay Ruth's old notebooks, also new works, she sent them all to him. He completely supervised her course of study. But all that was still not "Ruth."

He took a folder from the desk, in which all the letters from Heidelberg lay from the previous August to this April.

At first, they were all letters from Mrs. Römer. Ruth couldn't write, she was in a fever. They feared it was a lingering fever. Erik had been fully prepared for departure, he had already wired his arrival.

Then a telegram arrived, which held him back. Three days later, a short letter from Mrs. Römer:

"Your presence is not desired. The separation would result in the same thing again. Ruth must learn to live without you. Therefore, under no circumstances should you come. My husband means it as a doctor, but I mean it also – as a woman. I love Ruth like my own child; if you want to help me watch over her like a mother, then keep everything – even the slightest – that could awaken longing out of your letters."

A week later, Mrs. Römer wrote:

"Ruth is doing better. But yesterday she frightened us very much. In her room stands my armchair, covered with brown leather; she absolutely wanted it when she saw it at my place and said regretfully: 'What a pity it isn't green!'

Last night she had moved this chair to the middle of the room, opposite her bed. When my husband quietly entered to check on her, he saw Ruth sitting upright in bed, leaning forward, her eyes fixed on the chair, her face ecstatic.

When she saw my husband, she fell back into the pillows. 'Oh, – now he's gone!' she said sadly.

She was in a half-faint, cold all over.

We had to remove the armchair from her room. She insists 'it doesn't work' with the other chairs.

In sincere friendship, Irene Römer."

Soon after, the first note came from Ruth herself, still scribbled with a pencil from bed. Only a few lines, including a postscript:

"I believe that people could do magic if they wanted to."

In the folder, alongside this small note, was a letter from Erik's hand, – a complete draft, starting:

"My dearest child!

Besides the known ten commandments, there is an eleventh, especially for you: 'Thou shalt not do magic.'

In ancient times, when their gods did not fulfill the wishes of individuals, people sometimes resorted to all sorts of evil spirits, which could still be conjured up through magic and incantations. They might have done this for two reasons: out of cowardice or out of arrogance, out of a lack of belief that there was truly a wise, good power in the will of their gods, – or out of defiance, tired of obeying and trusting.

You don't do the same, – no matter for which of these reasons? You don't take behind-the-back and on your own authority what should be withheld from you? You don't call upon, like then, in the last night, a strange, evil spirit, the fever, to help you and lead you into a reality that is not one?

Thou shalt not do magic. Thou shalt surrender to the reality that surrounds you, – wholly, with faith and trust that you are at home in it –"

Here the letter draft broke off, the next lines were crossed out, – rewritten, and crossed out again. They had evidently been difficult for him to write.

But the drafts multiplied, following each of Ruth's letters; Erik impatiently pushed them aside: their presence spoke volumes.

His gaze lingered only longer when he encountered Mrs. Römer's fine, characteristic handwriting again. He could never entirely shake the feeling that he was in a secret, unconscious struggle with her – or she with him? – yet these letters refreshed him. If she was, unknowingly and unwillingly, an enemy, she was a magnificent one. One that should be wished for, to measure oneself against.

Around this woman, there was an atmosphere like clear, pure air, – one had to feel good in it. And every one of her words was such a clear expression of what she warmly felt. While reading, one believed to hear her voice, a cheerful, determined voice.

Erik was about to close the folder and put it back in its place when he noticed another letter from Ruth. Written many weeks ago and not more emotional than the others, – also, like the others, without greeting and without any other closing than "Ruth." But on the last page, there was a slip: suddenly, there was "Du" instead of "Sie."

She had vigorously crossed out the small betrayer and re-conjugated the verb. But in the margin of the page, it was honestly admitted: "I said 'Du,' but I meant 'Sie.'"

Erik never looked into the folder without lingering at this spot, – and he often looked into it.

This one syllable was her only real greeting to him. She would hardly ever have misspoken orally. She didn't need to. She had said "Du" to him every day, almost every hour, with her gaze and tone and demeanor. Only now did it become an understandable word, irresistible: a replacement for all wordless closeness.

Erik pushed the letters aside, wanting to work. To work, – anything but this unnatural, completely enervating existence in feelings and thoughts, – this uncertain groping into the blue, into the distance, with the renunciation of action. How easy the time of separation had been for him in comparison: innermost, most intense activity until the last second, the highest collected and enhanced power: for Ruth.

Now the backlash. Letting go, – letting go. It almost made him sick.

And he worked hour after hour until one blue school notebook after another was covered with the necessary red ink strokes.

Then he leaned back, tired, in his chair. And again he read, with ever new commentaries, the single syllable "Du."

The next day brought the first real spring feeling outside. A deep blue sunny sky shone over the bare trees.

A narrow, grayish, perforated snow crust still lined the edges of the gravel paths, but fresh, juicy green blades were already lifting from the dead grass, and long brown bud tips had been patiently waiting for weeks on the birch branches. The meadow ground behind the garden was entirely under water, reflecting the sky and sun, with scattered, broken ice floes floating around.

As usual now, Erik had work in the city all day, alongside his school teaching the voluntary lectures he conducted this winter, partly in his city apartment with adult participation, partly in an empty classroom of the girls' school.

Whoever came here no longer belonged to the school, or almost didn't. One could tell from the conversations that usually awaited him from his listeners. They no longer spoke of imaginary events, but of balls and parties and admirers who were likely not just figments of imagination. School matters never, unless something very sensational occurred, like this morning, when a little girl had fainted during morning prayers in the large school hall and remained lying, – an epileptic fit. They said just seeing it was contagious, yet most had stared at the convulsing girl on the floor, foaming at the mouth, as if hypnotized.

In the middle of this conversation, the latest arrival, stifling a yawn, was the pretty Vjera with her bold dark eyes. She had grown even prettier since her teenage pranks.

"Are you here again?" Erik's most diligent student called out to her. "I wonder why? Don't you mind that he always only has mockery for you?"

"And praise for you; I'd rather have my share," she replied convincingly. "Let him mock, it does him good, he's in a bad mood. Do you think your diligence makes him happy, my dear little goose?"

"No one can be more diligent," remarked one sitting on the window sill, crocheting, awaiting the lesson.

Vjera laughed maliciously: "Well, he might miss all sorts of other things painfully, – for example, intelligence. – – Dear God, what's the use of such effort?"

"Then why don't you stay away? You wanted to have what Ruth had, – you the most."

Vjera lay sprawled lazily, arms stretched along the back of the bench, glancing sideways into the small hand mirror someone had placed near the window, always surrounded.

"I don't believe he is with us as he was with Ruth," she murmured, "it would be pure deception. Either Ruth fooled us, – or we are – dumb. Do you really think Ruth meant it when she was so ecstatic and said: 'Oh – – beyond this lies the whole life?' We're still standing before the wall, – like a flock of sheep."

"Well, then go over."

"I will," Vjera replied curtly, – "today. Will you? With a single leap! But don't scream! You can jump after."

In no time, they crowded around her, burning with curiosity.

"What will you do?!"

She said nothing. She just lifted her face to them and slightly puckered her mouth.

"A kiss?!"

They were already screaming.

Then Erik entered. He noticed they were distracted but did not address it. Vjera perhaps read correctly in his eyes: "Like a flock of sheep." He missed Ruth among them, not because he loved her, but because she constantly spurred him on, demanded his presence of mind continuously. For her, he had to be at his best, never faltering.

Here, that was unnecessary.

After a short time, Vjera stood up and approached Erik with a piece of paper in her hand. "Could it be?" he asked sarcastically, assuming she wanted to present him with an assignment. "It would be the first time."

She climbed the two steps to the lectern and bent over him – so deeply that he looked up. At this movement of his head, their faces almost touched.

Then a scream pierced the classroom, in unison. They couldn't hold out.

But immediately followed a second, entirely different in tone: Vjera had fallen backward as soon as the first scream rang out.

Erik himself was confused about cause and effect, whether the first scream preceded or followed, – whether she bent down because she was falling. – He had heard about the incident in the school hall, and now the girls were seized by the memory of it with headless fear.

Most jumped up, some onto the benches, – onto the window sill.

Erik broke through. He lifted the seemingly lifeless girl in his arms and carried her out.

As he walked quickly down the hallway to the next empty room, she came to life. Her whole soft, supple body moved as if striving, trembling, to cling to him; her breath flew, and as if to hold on, she wrapped her arm around his neck, and now – now she clearly felt how it heated him.

In a flash, before he even realized, she pressed her mouth to his lips.

But in the next second, she found herself set on her feet – hard, so suddenly she nearly collapsed. He was seized by a senseless rage. A vision of the moment he had carried Ruth, like a lifeless child, to her bed stood before him.

He grabbed the bewildered imp by the wrist almost brutally and forced her the few steps to the tall double doors that closed off the hallway to the stairwell. He shoved the door open.

"Out! Without return!" he said curtly.

She blushed and paled. She only walked down slowly, step by step, holding onto the railing. What would the others in the classroom think if she didn't come back at all? That he had helped her over the wall? Yes, thoroughly. With one leap.

And the worst; she had a proper bump, right in the middle of her forehead. –

Erik struggled to regain control of his mood upon returning to his class, which tormented and depressed him. He had always wondered, seeing the pretty wastrel still sitting in her place with incomprehensible persistence, yet determined not to learn anything. He had also been a little pleased. Because she was a clever thing, full of wit and imagination. He now knew what kind of imagination.

But wasn't it his fault? Wasn't it his responsibility to unerringly guide all these young people? To cut out the excess, supplement the lacking, awaken the dormant? He had given himself to his task with his will, but not with his heart. And no willpower, however good, could replace his most powerful educational tool: the freshness and fullness of his spirit, whose ever-ready interest also dug into the smallest things, seeking, enticing, deeply understanding. And he needed this particularly. For his strengths and weaknesses as a teacher were that he could not separate his personality from his teaching; if he failed to give himself, everything failed.

At the school gate, Jonas waited for his father. They rode home together to the countryside.

In the train car, Jonas said, "Mama keeps talking about traveling soon. She can't go to the spa so early in the year?"

"I don't know yet. Maybe it will be desirable. In Germany, it's not so early in the year. The only thing against it is that I can't take her there myself now. You would have to do that, Jonas. And she would take Gonne."

"When I start studying medicine," Jonas remarked after a pause, "then I'll always have before my eyes the wonderful thing that Mama got better. I think: being a doctor and a single such case, – that must make one a happy person for life."

"You are a good boy, Jonas. – I didn't think you would specifically choose 'medicine.' I thought natural sciences."

"Yes, I did too, – earlier. Preferably zoology. But the future is so uncertain with it. A doctor always finds his bread."

"That's true. But that alone shouldn't be decisive. It still depends on the strength of special inclination and aptitude. At least for you. The other would be my concern."

"But I want to become independent as soon as possible, Papa. Self-sufficient."

"Is it so unpleasant for you to be dependent on me, my boy? It's only your good right. For a long time yet. I don't want your studies to be shortened or restricted by anything."

The rest of the ride, they were silent. Each looked out a different window, lost in their thoughts.

At home, over the garden, it was already darkening. Light blinked from the living room. The late afternoon, now falling into evening, awaited them.

As Erik entered, he placed a handful of pale blue lilac branches on the table. He had brought them in a silk paper wrapping.

"But Erik!" Klare-Bel said reproachfully, though she blushed with joy, "something so precious and unnecessary! In the Russian April!"

"Unnecessary?" He skillfully arranged the long stems in a cut glass vase. "Spring is not unnecessary. And I thought: in a country house, it must at least be inside if it's not outside."

Her eyes slowly filled with tears, which she lowered so he wouldn't see. Spring had indeed come inside, her spring, which she had awaited like a renewal of life just for Erik. But this spring had remained flowerless and frosty.

No, that was unfair. Unfair to him, to whom she owed her recovery: she glanced at Erik repentantly. But she had to see: he could hardly bear the separation, – the separation from Ruth. As long as Bel had seen him happy, she had remained unsuspecting and carefree. But now it weighed on her day and night.

"Have you answered Ruth's letter from yesterday yet?" she asked after a pause.

"Yes. But not completely," he replied.

She drew the lilac close and buried her face in the fragrant clusters.

"There was, – is the young Russian still there, whom they like so much?"

"Jurii? Yes. I think he's even supposed to stay with them for a short time during the upcoming holidays – out at the Schlossberg. They wanted to undertake various things together. Römer thinks highly of him."

A small pause ensued.

"How old is he actually, Erik?"

"About twenty-two, I think." "And entirely independent, right? It's not about a bread study for him?"

"No."

Erik looked up, a fleeting smile on his lips. Jealous of the young Russian, – no, he was not under any circumstances.

"A truly feminine combination, Bel. You already thought of a bridal wreath and veil, didn't you? But for Ruth to quickly become familiar with him, there is another reason: he is not a stranger to her. He knows her uncle here. Used to visit with his parents there, – played with her when she was eight, and he was thirteen."

She leaned back.

"It's nothing," she thought, "it can't be. Otherwise – he would have to be jealous. Despite his strong self-confidence. Youth seeks youth."

After a while, she said pleadingly, "Erik! You mustn't be angry. I have such a great wish."

"Such a bad one, Bel? Well, out with it."

"I long so much, – I would so very much like to read, just once, what you write to Ruth."

He didn't answer. He stood up and left the room. Shortly after, he returned with the almost finished letter in his hand.

"You can read it every time, Bel, if you want."

Her eyes shone at him so gratefully and joyfully that he couldn't bear the look. He looked away.

It was a pain for him to see her sitting there, – to see her reading. He would have preferred to leave.

He stepped to the window and looked into the darkness.

But the windowpane mocked him. What it reflected was once again the room with the lamp and the delicate lilac branches on the table and the reading woman in the armchair.

Klare-Bel let the letter sink. She looked startled.

"How strange, Erik," she said, "– I can't imagine you writing to Ruth like that."

"I don't think I write to her differently than I spoke to her," he replied.

"It may be. But then perhaps there was all sorts of other things that only exist in spoken words. Your whole being was added. You are so young and fresh in your demeanor, Erik."

"Well – and?"

He turned around. Surely Ruth found his letters just as "dreadfully dry" as he found hers. Only for a different reason: she couldn't express her inner self, – and he wasn't allowed to.

"Yes, – well, – I don't know how to describe it, Erik. But in the letter there you are like a venerable old man with long white beard and hair, – roughly like children imagine God."

It struck him. He had to think of Ruth's word: "Like God."

A multitude of conflicting emotions stirred in him. What made this correspondence dry for both him and Ruth, – cold and silent in the liveliest conversational tone, – were probably two entirely opposite feelings when reading the letters.

For him, it was a deduction from the fullness of the human, her personality, her innermost being, which could only show its surface in words. For her, it was perhaps an addition to his human personality, a transfiguration of it: after all, he had to keep his innermost being silent to her in person, and it was precisely that which she now perhaps idealized from his written words, – "roughly like children imagine God."

Hence, it had never occurred to him that she might have as much to criticize about his letters as he did about hers. For he had felt: in his letters, she took his hand and walked along trustingly. Obedient, – happy. For she did not suffer, did she? No, she certainly didn't.

They had surrounded her with a life that must constantly stimulate, enrich, develop her, – make her happy and fulfill her. And with her unlimited receptivity, she stood in the midst of this life, – as if with wide open arms.

No, she – she did not suffer.

Klare-Bel had also fallen silent. Again, each was lost in their thoughts, and again, it became a silent dinner. Though they sat closely together, in heartfelt affection, they were so worlds apart that none of them participated in the silent world of the other.

When Erik did not leave his room after dinner, Jonas sat with his mother, without schoolwork.

"If Papa isn't here, I must replace him," he assured, "can't I soon be almost the same as Papa for you? I'm already a good head taller than you, my little mama."

She looked at him with a deep, quiet gaze he didn't understand.

Then she stretched her hand over the table to him.

"My dear boy. Yes, you can soon be much to me. You won't forget it later, over all the studying? You must give me much, much joy, Jonas."

"I will give you a tremendous amount of joy, Mama," he declared sincerely, "that I will, for sure. Because I will become something quite extraordinary. I must."

"Are you looking forward very much to the new, unbounded life outside?"

"To outside – yes. But the unbounded life part I don't find so nice. I think it's much nicer the way Papa had it."

"How, my child?"

"Well, so completely bound, Mama. Together with you. Because I can imagine that so wonderfully. Almost as if –. A student room, – only small needs to be for the beginning, and books on the walls, and a cooker on the table for self-cooking. In the corner, a beautiful skeleton, and flowers in the window. There the wife sits with her sewing. And at the books, there I sit, – I mean: Papa sits."

"A small cradle?"

Jonas blushed. He hadn't thought of that part of the room's furnishings yet. He said somewhat awkwardly: "Well, yes. But even if you only sat next door, that was what made him diligent.

And that's what I think is so wonderful about studying when you do it for someone you love above all."

"Better not tell Papa that. It might displease him. That's not how he meant it with his studies and plans. He was so different from you, Jonas. But he was infinitely good and wise. And when he had to start worrying about bread, and it distressed me, he laughed so heartily and said: 'Let it be, Bel, I have a remedy, a magic remedy, to stay fresh, – no matter how much trouble there is, – fresh for my goals: the remedy is you, Bel.' Yes, that's what he said."

Jonas remained silent. He didn't want to belittle his father in front of his mother, but in this matter, he felt far superior to him.

"You can love a thousand times more!" he thought silently.

Klare-Bel's thoughts, however, dreamed themselves, painfully and joyfully, back to the time of their student marriage. She saw everything before her, as if she had just left it, and wandered through every corner that had housed their happiness. She also saw the room where he sat over his work, and she cared for him quietly – very quietly it had to be. But this image blurred, became indistinct as if through tears. In Erik's place sat another, – Jonas sat there; – and again, with a dull future fear, she saw herself alone, – alone with the son.

Klare-Bel lay awake at night, and as she was about to doze off towards morning, the thought startled her that she had to ponder something intensely and with pain.

The next day, school was canceled, some Greek church saint was being celebrated. Erik sat in the morning with some books and papers in the living room, where a desk had been improvised for him near the fireplace. Outside, a fine snowstorm blew from a few dark clouds, behind whose blue-black edge the April sun teasingly already laughed out. Light and dark glided over the room.

Klare-Bel's eyes hung on the working man with a wistful expression. This morning, she wanted to ask him. She couldn't stand it any longer. How had she only thought his letters would reveal him? For Ruth was still so entirely unaware. He couldn't speak openly to her. Hence, the notably reserved tone. He hid himself from her – awkwardly and laboriously.

"Where is Jonas, actually?" Erik asked, bent over his work.

"Jonas has gone to the city again. He wanted to visit his friend."

"Hopefully not to work again – with the friend?"

"Maybe. Let him, Erik. Hasn't he become excellent?"

"Yes, perhaps too excellent. He has achieved much, that must be conceded. Both in terms of his abilities and his perseverance, he has far exceeded my expectations in the last six months."

"Not just that. He has become so sensible. No nonsense in his head. No childishness."

"Yes. That's precisely what I dislike. For that, he is too young. He shouldn't be a philistine at seventeen."

"Oh Erik, as long as he becomes good."

"He can always become that. First, his temperament needs to come out! Heidelberg will do him good, I think, and Römer's influence. One must ensure he can move freely. Neither time nor money should be too tightly measured."

"How good he is!" thought Klare-Bel. "Yes, in such things, he has always been infinitely good. Would struggle for the boy, so he can learn to enjoy."

Several minutes passed in silence. Erik's thoughts ran ahead to the autumn when Jonas would go to Heidelberg. At the very latest then, he had to see Ruth again, speak to her. Perhaps even earlier. If Klare-Bel traveled to the spa in such a way that he could pick her up from Germany at the beginning of the summer holidays.

"Erik!" said a voice beside him.

He looked up, distracted. His wife stood by the desk – without her supporting sticks. She had risen without help and walked across the room to him – alone.

She had practiced it secretly for several days.

Erik couldn't immediately come out of his thoughts. He just looked at her questioningly, without noticing what should surprise him.

He didn't notice.

The smile on Klare-Bel's lips died.

"I just wanted to show you what I can do," she said, with a forced effort to sound casual.

But it failed. She turned pale. And suddenly, she swayed and slipped into the arms of the startled man who had jumped up.

He slowly led her to her armchair, concerned, bending over her. Now he was entirely with her.

"Are you better?" he asked warmly and pulled over one of the low upholstered chairs from the fireplace, "independence doesn't suit you, my poor Bel."

She looked at the jesting man with a long, silent gaze.

"I must learn it, Erik!" she replied ambiguously.

She leaned her head back tiredly and closed her eyes. And so, with closed eyes, while he held and gently stroked her hand, she said, "You see, – oh Erik, it was certainly very childish. But you see, – I had been looking forward to it for so long. To your joy, – if I could come to you like this – without support, on my own feet. It was so childish. But now I've lost all courage to ask you, Erik."

"What did you want to ask me, Bel?" he spoke with a suppressed voice, muffled as always when he suppressed an emotion.

"Yes, Erik, I thought: if you were so happy and embraced me, – not because I fell, but because I stood, upright beside you, – then I wanted to ask you, – very quietly, – oh Erik! I can't anymore!"

He took her hands in his and looked penetratingly, with the most intense attention, into the pale face with the tightly closed eyes. His heart pounded hard against his chest.

"I will tell you, Bel!" he replied firmly, without looking away from her. "If it has tormented you, then it must be. Do you have the courage to hear it? Do you want to?"

She opened her eyes, – helpless, tear-filled, – helpless like a trapped animal before the shot.

"Erik!" she whispered, and the horror of his answer enlarged her eyes, "–Erik, do you love her?"

Then he bowed his head deeply over her hands.

"Yes, Bel," he said aloud.

At that moment, a broad sunbeam flooded the entire room, so that Klare-Bel's lids closed involuntarily in a superstitious fright, as if heaven itself wanted to testify for Erik's love. Blue laughter shone down, and like a sparkling golden net of dew drops, the quickly melted snowflakes blinked over the garden. So warmly played the bright sunbeams over the lilac bouquet at the window, as if it had been cut from the bush outside.

"Dark," Klare-Bel whispered softly, "– I want to go to my bed, – make it dark."

He lifted her from the chair and laid her in her small adjoining room on her bed, drawing the curtains behind him.

She searched for his hand.

"The letters, Erik, – how you wrote to her, – was it all a pretense? Or did you, – didn't you write differently to her? Never?"

"I did write differently to her, Bel. Very differently. Every single time a letter like that went to her. But it was only for me alone. She never read it."

"You didn't send it? – Do you still have these letters, Erik?"

"No. I destroyed them every time as soon as they were written."

"Why did you do it then, Erik?"

"It helped me."

He almost added: "I love her, Bel! I love her! I had to speak to her."

After a while, Klare-Bel let go of his hand and said quietly: "And I had no idea, – no idea that you gave her up for that. Only now do I know."

He straightened up, struck. Did she misunderstand him now? Did she think he gave up Ruth for her sake? To master his love?

Did he have to inflict the last, the most mortal insult: "I did not think of you in that."

Yes, once that too must be. But did it have to be today? Everything today? Didn't she suffer enough, – immeasurably?

He couldn't do it.

As Klare-Bel no longer spoke to him, he stepped back from her bed to the open door of the living room.

It was horrible to strike down a defenseless person with a fist. Pity overwhelmed him with an unprecedented merciless power, – with an unprecedented painful, wretched feeling.

The fireplace crackled high under short gusts of wind; the sky had long since darkened again. A fine snowstorm swirled around the window once more, – the same April game as before.

Erik threw a handful of pinecones into the red glow, and a faint scent he loved like no other, – a scent of forest and Christmas spread in the room. Unintentionally, one thought of the bare, cold garden in winter frost and a decorated Christmas tree in the corner of the room.

Christmas, – – – also this winter, they had decorated the tree and gathered around it, but for the first time, they had felt like three poor adults, left out on the children's festival. Erik, who knew how to give like only Knecht Ruprecht, and to rejoice like only a child, had been stingy, – had remained reticent.

It seemed strange to him that his pity attached to such small, petty memories.

He slowly began to pace the room.

Not that she now lay and suffered, – but that she had waited so long, – long in vain for his joy, had searched his face for joy all these months, – that deeply moved him. She had recovered, – like a radiant Christmas tree, it should have stood among them at every hour, glittering, adorned with a thousand new little joys. And they had not gathered around it like happy children – –.

Klare-Bel still lay there in silence. He didn't want to go to her, he didn't want to leave. He still paced like a condemned man.

Finally, Jonas came. He sprang up the steps to the terrace and already held two letters high at the window. Entering the living room, he threw them on the dining table.

"Where is Mama? There was nothing else in the mailbox at the city apartment. Two for you."

"Mama is not feeling well. She is lying on her bed."

While Jonas tiptoed to the bed, Erik reached for the letters. One from Mrs. Römer, the other from Warwara. Without knowing why, he opened Warwara's short note first: the request to dine with her the next day, she asked for news about Bel's current condition and wished to also make a communication to him, she would be traveling abroad in about a week.

Erik sat by the window and opened Mrs. Römer's letter. A longer one than usual. Eight pages.

"Dear Friend!

Today I am writing on a special matter that concerns our Ruth. But do not be alarmed, for firstly, it is nothing alarming, and then it is also not a reality yet, but only a possibility for now.

You probably guess that it is about Jurii. I knew of his youthful infatuation for Ruth, without paying it much attention. Such things are ultimately not a disaster for a young person. But now I believe that he seriously loves Ruth and is about to propose to her. This is of little interest to you, unless Ruth loves him in return. For that, I have no solid evidence. But the strange thing is that one can never fully fathom what goes on in Ruth, and how she thinks in her innermost heart. I have never seen a person who is more open, never one who is more secretive than she. Open: consciously; closed: unconsciously. It is as if she still leads a secret inner life behind everything else that becomes visible, of which she herself is not quite aware, but from which all her decisive feelings and thoughts nevertheless come. So, she could very well act once to her own surprise, – to the surprise of her entire clear, fresh, cheerful unselfconsciousness, – and thereby express her truest self.

But now to Jurii. I can only report good things, even excellent things about him. I can only put it into words: if I had a daughter, – I would be pleased. He is good, sympathetic, very gifted, serious in the direction of his character and interests. Completely unspoiled. In addition, he is healthy to the core and a handsome young man. That is a lot at once. About his family and circumstances, you were already informed of the best yourself. His great youth is no flaw, as Ruth shares it with him and time so thoroughly heals it.

But please do not believe, despite everything, that my wishes precede Ruth's, – on matchmaker's feet. I only wished to prepare you in advance, so that you can consider how you want to approach the matter. Because against your will, – no, even just without your full will, – Ruth would never do anything."

Erik did not read further.

He skimmed the next pages: they no longer dealt with this.

Ruth's silence, – was it intentional, conscious? Turning away from him, a quiet transformation?

He did not believe his own awakening doubts. But they came back. Light and dark, brightness and shadow glided over his thoughts, like outside.

"April weather – within me! over a boy!" he murmured angrily, "in fear of an April whim, – in fear of being fooled in April!"

He was so angry, as unjust as possible against her, against himself.

Leaving his mother's room, Jonas saw his father walking into the snowstorm on the terrace.

And Klare-Bel wanted to rest, wanted to be alone. So he sneaked into his room.

When Erik came home after a few hours, Gonne remarked to him that the lady had gone to rest, she was ill.

He went to her.

She sat upright in bed; books lay on the table beside her. In her nightgown, her small cap on her hair, smoothly brushed back as for the night, she looked at him confused and fearful. As if she was afraid of him. As if she was ashamed before him.

He could not bear it. He bent over her, his face on her hands, and kissed them. "Bel, – Bel, – forgive me."

She tried to smile, it was a strange, weak, small smile that came out. And now she turned dark red.

"Oh Erik, – not like this. It is too – it is so unusual for me. It's terrible. Don't speak to me like that."

He sat down next to her, on the chair by her bed.

"Did you read, Bel?" he asked distractedly, tormented.

"Yes, Erik. You mustn't be angry about it. These are such old books, – the old ones, you know? But recently, I found something once, and it made me so happy. I looked it up today. It's so lovely to read, Erik."

She spoke quickly, awkwardly, like an embarrassed girl.

He looked down at the books. A golden cross on one. And the other: P. A. de Génestet's "Lay Poems," – these genuinely Dutch songs, in which defiance and faith, comfort and doubt mix oddly enough.

"I had completely forgotten them, both of them. I don't even know how. – How good that such things remain, even if one forgets them. They were so dusty and buried when I found them recently. – Will you hand me the 'Lay Poems,' Erik? There's a bookmark in it."

He opened the book and handed it to her. The bookmark fell out.

"Just listen, – Erik, – just a few verses, will you? You must find it beautiful too. It's called 'Peinzensmoede.' It should mean: 'I believe, Lord, help my unbelief.'"

And she read with her gentle voice:

"Where are the priests Who explained you? In riddles, man walks On earth. Mystery – life, Mystery – death, Creation preaches No loving God. Nature surrounds you, Which does not listen to you, Whether it does good, Or destroys.

And yet, – doubts nest In my chest, – I believe in you, my Father, Unconsciously. Not because your creation Reveals your love, – No! no! only despite everything, Despite the doubt! Despite every riddle, Despite every need, Despite fear and destruction, Despite pain and death!

I languish, struck down By fate, My hope is melancholy, My melancholy is hope. I want to – want to believe, That I felt your hand In life, Only did not recognize it; – Want to believe, what church And priest taught me: That no one sought you In vain on earth."

She sat and read, her head with the white nightcap devoutly bowed, her hands folded on the blanket. The blush of awkwardness, the embarrassed expression slowly faded from her face, looking touching and trusting, like a child reciting a prayer to its mother.

And so nakedly she still laid her soul before him, in all its helplessness and timid hope, – without any false pride. She knew no other way.

Erik still held the bookmark and absentmindedly examined it. A rather inappropriate one had found its way into the book: a naked Cupid with a large bouquet of roses.

As he silently stared at it, he spoke to Klare-Bel in his mind, interrupting her reading, taking the book from her hand. He was entirely absorbed in this wordless conversation:

"This title surely does not belong over your faith and your doubts, Bel; 'Peinzensmoede' means: tired of brooding. When did you ever know that? A loosely draped garment, – a garment that loosely slipped off you by chance in your marriage: that was faith in your life."

And in his thoughts, he heard Klare-Bel: "But what else should I believe in, Erik? In you? Not in you, surely? Where should I find support? You were my support! Oh, that doesn't hold! It bends away under my hand and lets me fall. Should I harm myself? Murder you? Poison her? I am not one of those people who are crushed by passions. Does that make me only more helpless? My deepest despair is helplessness, – the groping for support: my last clear thought. Why do you deny it to me?"

"Because I hate this support, – this hold that is supposed to replace me. No, because I am ashamed of it, – that it must replace me. Because I have no more pity for you, – only anger and shame before myself."

Klare-Bel looked up from her book, made uncertain by his silence.

"Isn't it beautiful, Erik?" she asked softly, almost pleadingly, "– it makes me happy."

"Then it's beautiful, Bel!" he said gently.

But his mood was not gentle. All evening, he struggled with a pain unfamiliar to him. Already in the morning, – when he had not immediately clarified her misunderstanding but let her believe him nobler than he was, – and now again, where his lips spoke differently from his ashamed, angry thoughts, – he had acted against his innermost nature, passively, letting things go. Not out of a softness of pity, – out of just conviction: whether it was sympathetic or repulsive to him should not matter against what Klare-Bel had to suffer through him.

He had inevitably brought himself to the point of having to act against his innermost nature.

The next day, Erik required a violent exertion of will to tear his thoughts away from everything that tormented him and focus on his work. Soon he saw Bel as a praying sister, soon Ruth as a bride; mockery and bitterness filled him. In both cases, he was the dethroned king.

"A new god for one, – a new man for the other, – it's almost the same!" he thought and was himself horrified by the ugliness of his thoughts.

During a break between his school hours, while calling at his city apartment, he pulled out Mrs. Römer's letter from his pocketbook. He had not even read it all, – just skimmed it, – and now he felt: it must do good to hear this woman's voice, to find peace with her from all the ugly things that can be stirred up in a person.

And he read on:

"It's not necessary for Ruth to bind herself so young. Perhaps she will marry much later, – perhaps never. Now see, this would not be desirable. I don't know how you think about it. I speak as a happy woman naturally for marriage. But I have an easy time talking: without my husband, I would have remained a worthless thing, – with some interest in trifles and a great emptiness in my heart. I believe you place primary value on Ruth's intellectual development. I do too. But a happy early love life is not a contradiction, but the only healthy, natural basis for intellectual striving in women. Not just so she can be the man's helper. Often, it doesn't suffice for more. But where it does, – all the better. I am certain my husband would have supported me in pursuing any profession where there was corresponding great aptitude. Not out of pure selflessness, of course. Love is not selfless. But to have the whole fresh fragrance, the whole fullness and joy around him, which only a fully blossomed person radiates to their surroundings. And that two blossoms want to stand next to each other: that probably means 'marriage.'"

Erik jumped up and threw the letter on the table.

Something entirely different from what he had sought he had found in it, – something completely unexpected: an unconscious reproach.

His marriage to Bel, those were not two independent blossoms standing together: that was a blossom that had absorbed a dew drop that had carelessly fallen into its cup.

That's probably how Mrs. Römer would express it.

The Römers stood differently from the start. They admired each other, – actually, it was touching. One couldn't quite smile about it: one had to respect these two people.

Bel couldn't be compared to Mrs. Römer. When he found her, a year older than himself, stunningly beautiful, already finished with her short development, – in a certain way, a much more finished person than he, – what else could he have done but absorb, thirstily, what offered itself, longing for self-extinction?

But when you take such absolute possession of a weaker person, you feel the terrible obligation not to separate from them again. You place yourself for life in a struggle between shame and pity at every slightest attempt to free yourself from this obligation.

That would probably be Mrs. Römer's opinion. – Also – Ruth's opinion? Ruth didn't brood over such questions. But what acted on her daily, hourly, more powerfully than all words, all brooding, – that was Mrs. Römer's marriage. A holy, happy marriage.

As soon as his teaching allowed, Erik went to Warwara. More than he wanted to admit to himself, it was right for him not to return home just yet.

When Erik was announced, a tall, gaunt Englishwoman, Warwara's companion, left the room.

"You look particularly serious," he remarked when greeting Warwara, "nothing unpleasant has happened to you in the meantime, has it?"

She had to laugh out loud.

"Something has happened, – yes. But one doesn't count it as unpleasant."

"– Engaged?! – was that the announcement?! – To whom?"

She sat in her chatting corner. "It doesn't matter to whom. A complete stranger to you. You will read it on a nicely engraved engagement card."

"And may I wish you happiness, Warwara?"

"How do you mean that?"

"I mean, of course, whether you feel the slightest for the man you want to marry."

"You doubt it."

He was silent.

"I will tell you. That's why I called you here. I like him. Very much. But I don't get hot and cold thinking about him."

"And that seems to suffice for you. It does not suffice, Warwara."

"So I will confess more to you. What I seek in marriage, – the happiness I seek, – is not the man."

"What then?"

She stood up and stepped to her flower table, busying herself with the plants. "The child."

Erik was surprised into silence.

After a short pause, she said: "It is a very intimate confession. But I am very intimate with you, – more than you know. Often asked you in silence for advice on various things. Made you my confessor and soul guide. We should have shared serious matters with each other more often than we did."

"That would have made me very happy, Warwara. Even what you are saying now makes me happy. I needed just that."

"Well, you see, that's good. So I will openly admit it. That I am really just a very poor worldly child, full of all sorts of trinkets and junk. And that I would like to be more. Maybe thanks to you, – thanks to the silent conversations I sometimes had with you. And so I now desire and wish for the only educator and master who can still make the best out of me, – the best that is in me."

"You expect all that from a child?"

"From motherhood, – yes. From mother love. Mother happiness. Mother duty. – And then," she turned to him lively, "sometime, if I am really so fortunate, then I will place my child in your hands to help raise it to be a capable person, you teacher of people."

"Would you have that much trust in me? Such firm faith in me? Thank you, Warwara."

"Yes. I trust you and your strength immensely. Under the one condition: that you love your task very much."

"In other words: no strength for duty loyalty."

"I don't know. I only believe, despite everything, that you are at heart a person of feeling. And that means: able to love very much – people or ideas, – and where one loves very much, able to give oneself completely. However, all the other things you sometimes confidently claim, – all the certainty and infallibility outside these guiding and decisive feelings, – no, – I don't believe in that either, even for you."

"You have become a great philosopher," he remarked softly.

"What? You admit it to me?" she asked surprised. "What foreign good spirit of yielding has come over you? But it is true, why should you not also feel at times how dependent we all are on happiness, – we poor worldly children all? On the fertile patch of earth where a whole happiness, a whole love, and – only through that! – also a whole duty and sanctity can grow for us."

"And if we are not allowed to cultivate this patch of earth, precisely this one?"

"Then we wither, – or we squander ourselves. At least I do. And you too."

A servant appeared in the porter's door and invited them to dinner.

Warwara stood up.

"Give me your arm. So serious? I did not hurt you?"

"No. You are absolutely right. You were right when you once said to me long – very long ago: 'We have a common temptation.' To recognize it means to become hard – against everything that prevents us from living out fruitfully."

In the countryside, Klare-Bel and Jonas sat next to each other at the table. Jonas found: sitting opposite each other was too formal. He enjoyed serving her and laying out for her, the best of everything. He made an effort to entertain her.

Klare-Bel didn't really listen, her eyes were fixed on a letter Jonas had brought with him. It had arrived after Erik's visit to the city apartment.

From Ruth. Completely out of time. Klare-Bel couldn't suppress a weak, foolish hope that intruded into Jonas's harmless chatter.

When Erik arrived home shortly after the evening tea, he immediately noticed the letter waiting for him. His glance brushed Jonas, – fleetingly only, – but Jonas immediately stood up to leave the room. The father knew very well how difficult that was for him, – but he didn't want to be accused of lack of self-control again, like that night before Ruth's departure. Jonas now obeyed him blindly, – at a nod; for even if he sent him out of the room: he still led him the way to Ruth.

Klare-Bel's eyes were fixed on Erik with unspeakable tension as he opened the letter. One single second, – the page turned, – another, lightning-fast, – and he balled the paper in his hand.

He was gray in the face.

"Erik! What is it? – something bad, – bad for you, – Erik!"

She was horrified by the changed expression on his face.

Erik unfolded the paper again, only his hand balled. Four words buzzed in his thoughts: "I love him," and at the end something like "I gave him the kiss," – he hadn't read more. He clenched his teeth.

To read this now, in front of his wife's eyes –

He read it, standing upright, brightly lit, in front of the lamp.

"At Schlossberg. Tuesday.

Mrs. Römer says I should write to you about Jurii. Whether I love him. I love him. And I should tell everything as it happened. It happened like this: It was storming and raining around Schlossberg. I wasn't allowed to go down to the city because I had been in bed with a cough. But I went anyway to get a book for my work. Downstairs I found Jurii, and he brought me home. We walked under an umbrella and had to huddle together. But it was very slippery, and Jurii had to keep making sure I didn't slip with the galoshes. Then Jurii said to me: 'I love you. I love you very much. Will you, please, be my wife?' But he said it in Russian, and I started to laugh because we always speak German. Then he said: 'I know now that you do not love me back. Then there is no more happiness in the world. I want to die.' Because he wanted to die, I became very sad, and so did he. We didn't pay attention to the umbrella and the galoshes anymore, I lost one, and the rain ran down our backs. Mrs. Römer scolded a lot when we arrived soaking wet, put me to bed, and made hot tea. I lay and cried because I didn't know how to make us happy again. At the same wall, someone lay on a couch in the next room, doing the same. Mrs. Römer came in and listened if someone else was crying next door, smiled a little, and said we were real children. Then she sat by my bed and stroked my hair back (she does it just like you) and asked if I didn't love Jurii a little. I said: 'Yes.' Then she said: 'I mean it differently. Think about what is the most beautiful thing in the world for you? Does Jurii belong to it?' I thought about it and said the most beautiful thing in the world was that I was your child. Then she said: 'Maybe now still. But can't you imagine that it would be much, much more beautiful later to be a bride for someone else's sake?' I couldn't imagine that. Then she didn't ask anymore. She kissed me and left.

Today Jurii left. He doesn't want to study here anymore. I was just with my many pots of snowdrops that I planted in the greenhouse in February. I cut the blooming ones for Mrs. Römer's vase so she would be kind again. Then Jurii came into my room. He wanted the flowers and a kiss. He looked so pale and tearful. I gave him the flowers. And I gave him the kiss too.

That is how it was.

Ruth."

Klare-Bel had turned her eyes away from the reader. His face revealed everything that was in the letter. Too clearly, it revealed that his fright had been groundless.

Seeing Erik in this dependency on what Ruth did or didn't do, – that was terrible. She did not want to see that.

She had thought the worst had come over her yesterday. But not knowing was the hardest, – no, seeing it with knowing eyes, daily, hourly, confirmed in such small events. To see this loving and wavering, – that was harder. Not just harder, – it was impossible.

And then, – if Ruth rejected another, – then she probably loved Erik too. And if she loved him, – then he was lost to Bel. He might be able to give up his happiness – for Bel, but never Ruth's happiness. Not if he truly loved her. Where the stronger love blooms, there also grows the stronger sense of duty: there one only cares for the other's happiness.

So Klare-Bel felt.

The next day, she was absent at the morning breakfast. Gonne had to bring it to her in her room.

Erik sought her out immediately. He had already risen very early and, after several failed attempts, written to Ruth.

But this time it turned out poorly, – a tone of torment ran through it.

Klare-Bel lay in her dressing gown on her former resting chair, a fur blanket over her knees. She did not look ill. Much more clear and collected.

"You are not feeling unwell?" he asked nevertheless, with sincere concern.

"I am not unwell, Erik. But I had to have you with me. Alone, – completely alone, – without Jonas."

And she clasped his hand with both of hers.

"To ask you: let me leave now! Already now. It was supposed to be soon anyway. Let it be now!"

He was silent for a moment. This request was eloquent. "If you absolutely want it, Bel. Then it shall be hurried. I will take care of every concern. I am bound now. But Jonas will take you."

"Oh no, Erik! Let me go alone. Not with Jonas. Gonne suffices. I ask you so much for this. With Jonas, I am not alone. He has such keen eyes. Before him, I don't want to –"

She broke off, but the only pride she had, her motherly pride, screamed within her: "Before him, I don't want to show my weakness, my misery!"

"Well then. Also that. He shall only take you across the border. On that, I insist, Bel."

"Thank you. And now I must tell you the other thing, Erik."

"What is it?"

He paced restlessly a few times through the room and leaned against the window. She spoke so clearly and so calmly, consciously. He knew his Bel completely, – knew every slightest movement in her, – and influenced her. And now an unknown, alien quality emanated from her being, – something foreign. He felt it, without yet being able to explain it to himself, like a pressure on his nerves. A very strange feeling: as if a third person were in the room.

"I just want to say it quickly, Erik. The other thing is that you should travel too, – as soon as possible. Not only in summer, to pick me up. Soon, – earlier, – during the Easter holidays. When you have two weeks off. To see her again. To convince yourself whether perhaps she –. Certainly, you must do that. For otherwise, you will be unhappy for life, Erik. And that, – you see, – I couldn't endure."

The flush had risen to his face. Dark red up to his forehead. He threw his head back against the windowpane.

That was it: she already had a new support that taught her to walk and act independently! A new master: she was already acting on his command!

How could he have thought of a struggle – with Bel! Struggle? No, he wanted to rob her, plunder her! But she wouldn't allow it: she gifted her robber, – willingly, over-abundantly gifted him: "Take, you poor dependent on happiness, – I can spare it, am the stronger, – I can renounce, – you – cannot."

And burning shame flared up in him, – burning shame, – and defiance as the only answer: "A thousand times rather a robber than a beggar!"

Klare-Bel did not look at the silent, speechless man. She was so completely absorbed and overwhelmed by the severity of what she intended that her eyes did not seek, did not question him, as they once would have.

"Last night, I kept thinking: if it were otherwise possible! But that's it: it's not possible. You can't stop thinking of her, and I, – how could I – how could I not start to hate her? And so we sin against each other, Erik. That must not be. Everything between us has always been beautiful. It can become sad, – terribly sad. But not ugly. That it mustn't. I couldn't bear it."

A half sound escaped him. She, – what did she know of "hatred"? Of ugliness. No, nothing! It filled him with an almost reverent wonder: in her, thoughts did not become ugly, not bitter and unjust, in the struggle and doubt, in the turmoil and wavering of the soul. She thought nothing ugly.

"And now I have also understood, – last night, – why I became healthy," Bel said quieter, as he still remained silent, "and why we couldn't be happy about it. Not happy, although I could stand and walk on my own feet. God spoke to me in it: 'Go!'"

"Bel!" he exclaimed tormentedly. This religious exaltation was terrible to him. But Klare-Bel said calmly, almost kindly: "Yes, Erik. And I go. God Himself wanted it so. He wanted it. But Jonas you must leave me later. Leave him with me. Jonas belongs more to me than to you."

Highest and most everyday things were mingling. Erik found: now she spoke of separation and parting like a house move; "this is more mine, – this more yours."

He stepped to her bed.

"Listen to me now, Bel. You make no decision – about anything, – before I have spoken to you now. Openly. More openly than before. For you do not know everything."

"Oh Erik, – don't say anything! It is terrible to hear it! – Nothing, – no! Only one thing – I would have asked from you!"

He took the hands she held out to him and gently held them.

"It must be, Bel. You must hear me."

"Wait. Please, not! Erik, – just tell me first: – did you – already write to her?"

"Yes," he replied, astonished.

"I mean – the other letter?"

"Yes, – also the other one."

"And you destroyed it. Didn't you, – didn't you?"

In that moment, he did not know it himself. Unconsciously, he reached into his jacket pocket. It crackled faintly under his fingers.

"Erik! – that is the only thing, – I would have asked from you."

His hand clenched around the thin, crumpled paper, – again a wave of blood rose to his face, – again the blush of shame, a fine, sensitive shame. No, – not that! That he couldn't! To expose the innermost, most secret, – his holiest and unholiest, – the turmoil of the wildest hour, – the devotion of the quietest – before Bel's eyes.

But only for a moment did he hesitate so. She was right, – a thousand times she had a right to it! And what she learned from it, she had to learn, – what she feared to learn. And if it was more than his confession could have expressed, – if it was himself with everything that raged, fermented, sobbed, fought within him, – with all the ugliness too, and the outcry for happiness, – then it was good that way.

She shied away from his words, – from the final clarity: and she reached into this darkness, demanding, – boldly. Who can fathom a woman's soul's fear and curiosity!

He handed her the crumpled sheet, – balled up into a wad.

"You wanted it."

Then he left her.

Next to him in the living room, the breakfast table was still set. Jonas had waited in vain for his father and had to go to school.

Erik stood in the middle of the room and stared into the void.

"Not to renounce!" was his only clear thought. "Not to renounce! not in the temptation of pity, – not in the worse one: the temptation of shame."

It felt to him as if it was not about a single person, not even a woman, – no, about everything that was human, what could be human for him, – about everything he could still touch, create, love, – about his own humanity.

It now concentrated in these two childlike, believing eyes that looked up to him and waited.

Renunciation meant going into the desert – not only with his love, – also with his creative power, – with his strength altogether, – into the unfruitful, into the dead loneliness.

Was there a strength even for the desert? That could withstand such loneliness? Yes, perhaps it arose in it? That no longer needed another, to remain strong and beautiful, – no eyes that believed and waited and appealed to it?

Yes, perhaps! for people of reflection, who looked over their own shoulders, reflected on themselves – mocking or enjoying! Or for people of feeling, who knew how to indulge and swim in their own emotions sentimentally, – also their own audience!

VI.

But not for those who are indivisibly one within themselves and therefore helpless in themselves—unless they can help themselves by acting, by working out of themselves—and recognizing themselves, reflected in the eyes of another.

But Bel? Why could she renounce? She, who neither indulged in reflections nor in feelings, she, who was rather naive and sober and not at all her own audience? But it also worked: with the great suggested spectator—up there, who saw everything. She too had her mirror, for which she had to keep herself beautiful—the eye of God, the blue sky mirror!

A faint sound, like a stammer or a groan, came from Klare-Bel's small adjoining room. It was as if she wanted to interrupt Erik in his bitter thoughts—contradict him.

He stepped to the open door.

Bel had thrown the letter away, far away, onto the lower edge of the fur blanket. She lay there, her face flushed red, buried in her hands.

"Dear God!" she prayed, "great, merciful God, who is in heaven and sees into the hearts of men: take my love out of my heart!"

•

Warwara was very surprised when she met Erik on the street the next day and heard about his wife's imminent departure. She spoke most animatedly, urging him to wait just one more week and then let Klare-Bel travel with her. But it was of no use. The very next morning she could place a mighty bouquet of roses in the carriage window for the departing woman, who promised her an early visit at the spa. Besides Erik, Warwara was the only one to accompany the mother and son, and she found that the spouses did not behave quite naturally towards each other.

After the train had left, Erik bade her a brief and hurried farewell. She drove home very thoughtfully.

Her clever thoughts completely misunderstood him. She actually believed him to be satisfied as a man in his own home, but dissatisfied as a person in his sphere of influence. And when she, jokingly or seriously, spoke of "temptations" for him, she meant occasional attempts to numb the hungry vitality with trifles and dalliances. Was something like that at play now? Now, when Erik lived so completely withdrawn—for a year already? When he had entirely disappeared from the brilliant, easy-going world of society that once captivated him and which he had captivated? Was a woman involved?

A few days later, on a Sunday morning, Warwara wanted to use a necessary inspection of her country house as an opportunity to call on Erik and find out if Jonas had come home with good news from the border.

As she boarded the first class of the Finnish train, she was surprised not to find herself alone. In the corner opposite her sat a very young lady, looking out the window with large expectant eyes.

Warwara regarded her with fleeting interest. As always, individual externalities struck her first and foremost.

A delicate, slender figure; the tightly fitting dark blue cloth dress with an open jacket part, lined with deep red English flannel, showed only a small white linen strip high at the neck. An impatiently moving narrow foot peeked out from under the skirt. Ash-blonde hair, held together in a knot by a strong tortoiseshell pin, protruded somewhat tousled around her forehead and temples from a soft dark blue velvet beret.

An indefinite memory arose in Warwara; she did not know of whom. A young Englishwoman? She stared so intensely at her counterpart that the latter turned slightly bewildered towards her.

For a few seconds, the young girl returned her gaze firmly and inquisitively. Then she greeted with a faint smile.

The smile suddenly put Warwara on track.

"Ruth!" she exclaimed. She immediately corrected herself, laughing. "Forgive me. The impertinence first and now. But I searched and searched, and what I found was what remained in my memory. Your first name."

"It is quite enough," Ruth said. "I assume we have the same destination?"

"No!" Warwara replied quickly, not wanting to intrude, "I am only going to inspect my country house that needs repairs. But our friends are expecting you?"

Ruth blushed and shook her head.

"No, I left Heidelberg very—quite unexpectedly," she replied with notable embarrassment.

A suspicion flashed through Warwara like lightning. "That is she, the 'temptation'," she thought, "very young, but I suspected even then behind her practiced forms: very cunning."

"Then you will be sorry to find a gap," she remarked aloud, "because you probably do not yet know that you will not meet Klare-Bel? She has already left."

"No!" Ruth exclaimed, shocked, "I couldn't have known! Is it for a bad reason? Yes, that is a shame!"

She looked so honest with her impatiently questioning eyes that Warwara felt ashamed. "She really didn't know, it wasn't planned, what a horrible person I am!" she said to herself and turned to Ruth with a heartfelt tone. "No, no bad reason. Klare-Bel is as healthy as one could never have expected, and now she is steadily improving.

At the beginning of winter, she still had to endure a lot. Once she said to me in gloomy jest: 'Erik has to force me violently to want to get well.' The man has iron in his blood. But it shook him up considerably. I saw him a few times: pale as a sheet."

Ruth listened silently, her hands clasped in her lap, her lips half open, her eyes only saying: "More!" When Warwara fell silent, she breathed deeply.

"He can do anything he wants! And he wanted it so wholeheartedly that she should be well and happy again. He lived for it. How infinitely happy they must be now! Now that he has guided everything to the good! Now that it is as he wants: where she is happy."

She spoke passionately, her eyes sparkling.

Warwara regarded her thoughtfully. She no longer seemed so formally polished and adept as back then, but on the contrary, like a being in whom everything was inner life, and nothing was form anymore. A soul, filled to the brim with devotion and faith—and love? Then she couldn't speak with such childlike innocence and joy. No love? Then she couldn't speak with this look and this tone.

The train stopped. They got off.

Warwara condescended to use one of the small rattling vehicles waiting at the station building, whose drivers immediately shouted at her. Ruth had a different path. So they parted.

As she drove off, Warwara repeatedly looked back at her.

"There is something there that does not belong to life—poetry. Poetry in conflict with life—what does that yield?" she thought; "it is as if one had turned the first page of a novel—oh, fie, no!— or: the last page of a fairy tale."

Ruth walked slowly between the bare birches along the roadside, not in a hurry to arrive a few minutes earlier. With a listening expression, she breathed in the spring around her as if it stood around her in a thousand blossoms. It wasn't there yet, it couldn't be seen—and yet it was there, in the air, in an all-encompassing invisible presence. It could be heard: in single fine little singing voices, it sang from the leafless branches.

The sky was slightly overcast, the sun shone down with subdued radiance—tone, light, color acted muted, veiled, and like a promise.

And now Ruth stood at the old wooden fence with the creaking gate. She opened it, crossed the garden, and climbed hesitantly, quietly, a few steps up to the terrace.

Leaning forward cautiously, she peered into the wide window of the living room to see if anyone was there.

The table was set for a second breakfast, behind the plates with cold fish and meat-filled pastries, the samovar steamed.

Jonas sat alone by the fireplace. He held a long roasting fork in his hand, on the prongs of which a slice of bread was stuck, and let it roast over the red wood embers. As he sat there, one arm lazily draped over the back of the chair, in a waiting posture, his head with the slightly too tightly closed lips brightly illuminated by the fire, he strongly reminded her of Erik.

The slice came too close to the flames; it suddenly slipped from the fork and fell in.

Jonas looked puzzled. He turned around and skewered a new one; this time it went better.

Then he expertly rinsed a teapot with hot water and made an infusion. In doing so, his fingers clumsily got under the open spout of the samovar, and a boiling stream scalded his hand.

Jonas opened his mouth wide and began to dance on one leg in the room.

Loud laughter sounded from the window.

He stopped as if a lightning bolt had struck him from the ceiling. With a disbelieving expression, his eyes, as if they did not trust themselves, turned to the window.

He stretched out his hands towards the image behind the closed pane, which laughed at him and looked like Ruth; he did not know whether he was dreaming Ruth or seeing Ruth.

But in the next moment, he had already thrown open the window so that it almost shattered, and his hands reached out for the laughing head and held it tight.

"But Jonas! Let me come in through the door first!"

"No—not!" he murmured, as if she could still suddenly vanish like a dream image, "Don't turn away, I won't let you! Through the window! It has to work. Set your foot on the ramp—very firmly—do you hear? I'll lift you."

She looked at him: that he said just like Erik.

She hadn't unlearned climbing. In one leap, she stood in the room.

He let her go. He stepped back. Now, when she stood before him, no longer behind a closed pane, his arms sank. A boundless shyness suddenly overcame him.

"How is it possible that you are here—where did you come from?" He stared at her as if convinced she had fallen from heaven.

"By the express train. Yesterday evening.—And—your papa?"

"He should be here. But now he forgets the time. Long walks he takes, alone—since Mama's departure."

"Oh Jonas,—that Mama has recovered—isn't it like a miracle—still?"

"Yes. And now I will become a doctor too. Do you know? In case you get sick later."

She had sat down by the fireplace and looked at him with joyful, mischievous eyes.

"I hope I will get sick later.—How have you been, Jonas? You never wrote."

He looked red and confused.

"Never? Me? But I had to—I thought—You! Don't you want a cup of tea?"

"No, thank you," she said, laughing, "but the main thing is: you are coming to Heidelberg soon, right? How wonderful, Jonas! Then we will study together."

"Yes," he replied, breathing deeply, "—finally!—soon! finally! finally together! Yes—you see: it couldn't have gone on much longer.—I've lived like in a grave," he continued with sudden vehemence, "—must be near you, Ruth.—With you. Yes—you!—I love only you. Only you I love,—don't take it amiss—but I really love you. I can't do anything, have nothing, am nothing,—I have to fight my way through first—but at least I want to be near you,—show my fist to anyone who wants it too,—who wants to come near you! Everyone! Let him beware! Knock down everyone—"

"Jonas! You're raving!"

She had jumped up, pale with fright.

He came to his senses, tried to smile, to smooth things over—and suddenly he fell to his knees before her, his face buried in the folds of her dress.

"Oh Ruth! Don't be angry! You don't know—it was so terrible for me—all the time—everything choked silently inside me. Look at me, don't be angry! Never again—it will never happen again, until—. I know—I can't yet. But once—once I had to—I would have suffocated otherwise. Oh, dear Ruth! I am so endlessly unhappy until—until you are—mine—mine!"

"Jonas!" she whispered, "—Jonas, please,—stand up,—let me go,—you are insane, Jonas! This can't be—"

He clung to her cloth skirt, which she tried to free from his fingers—he clung to her hand, her hip.

"It can't?!" he almost shouted, and as she freed herself with an unexpected movement, he mindlessly buried his teeth in the back of her hand.

Dark blood oozed forth.

She had thrown her head back and was silent.

He stood up slowly, coming to his senses. He kissed her hand.

"Forgive me," he said softly and helplessly broke into tears. "Ruth!—Don't you love me at all? Not a little bit? What—what are we to each other? what—in the future?"

She grasped him by the shoulders—anxiously and lovingly she looked into his disturbed face.

"Jonas! Now—and in the future—and always—siblings!"

He took her hands from his shoulders, walked slowly the few steps to the door, opened it—and dashed out, across the terrace, down the steps, and disappeared into the garden.

Suddenly it became deathly still in the house. Only the sparks crackled and flared brightly in the fireplace.

Ruth leaned against the table and looked down at the drops of blood on her hand. Slowly she blushed, deeper and deeper until her entire face was aflame.

What was she doing here—alone—in the house, an intruder, who had driven Jonas away?

The door had remained wide open. As if it said: "Go away again."

Ruth looked around. No, no one said that. Not even Klare-Bel. Only her large chair stood there, with a high footstool in front of it—empty.—

●

A short time later, when Erik opened the garden gate, Ruth was sitting at the far end of the garden, which the bare trees allowed a wide view, on the bench under the overhanging birches.

Erik stopped, looked more closely, and came slowly closer. She did not move. As if conjured by his longing into the gray spring, she sat there—in uncertain outlines—then increasingly warmer, increasingly animated before his eyes, no longer a pale thought image. Reality. Softly, the blonde head stood out from the whitish birch trunks and the wood behind them, which the sun penetrated dimly in a play of shadows of rosy-violet colors.

Ruth was paralyzed by a weakness, the closer Erik came to her, the closer the reality embraced her, the indescribably longed-for. "Home! Only now: home!" she thought as if in a dream, and her hands lifted toward him.

This strangely still, this inability to any outburst, any loud movement, also held Erik back—as if he feared to frighten away what he finally saw so eloquently, so wordlessly eloquent and convincing before him: gaze, expression, gesture.

Above Ruth's head, a robin perched on a swaying branch and sang brightly.

When Erik stood in front of the bench, it fluttered away in fright and flew off.

He had taken Ruth's hands, he held them firmly in his, he drew her hands tightly to himself.

"Dear—darling!" he murmured, his gaze on her face.

"I—the letter—it frightened me," she said faintly, "something foreign—doubt was in it. I had to leave."

He heard only her voice; he had to hear it again.

"Flew here with the robin?" he asked.

She looked at him—somewhat shyly, somewhat boldly. "Ran away," she said.

He sat down beside her, without letting go of her hands.

"From the Römers?!"

"I had to. They wouldn't let me. Römer helped me. But she—she remained adamant. How horrified she was. 'Not now!' she kept saying. So I ran away. Still by night—secretly. Sent a telegram on the way. I had to come.—Did I have the right?"

She asked it shyly, anxiously seeking his belated permission, like a child. She had pleaded on her knees before Mrs. Römer—but she didn't say that.

He took off her beret-like cap and brushed the hair back from her face. He had to see her completely again.

"Did you have the right?—Coming home—yes! By day and by night, secretly and openly. It was time. Two weeks later I would have come—to you. Forget the letter—all letters—the foreignness, the doubt—forget everything—everything. Just be with me."

Yes, there it was: the feeling of security, sweet, compelling, a feeling of home—no, more than just that, something else—this unconditional and exclusive feeling, which no power in heaven or on earth gave her: only he, alone.

"What happened to your hand? Injured? Let me see," he noticed and wanted to untie the handkerchief. She recoiled. "Does it hurt so much?"

"No. Nothing. Please don't," she said hastily, and a shadow passed over her happiness.

Erik stood up.

"Come inside. Come, darling. You are truly at home in my room—in the old leather chair—right? And it's still too cold for you here, too windy."

As they walked towards the house, Ruth said, "On the way, by chance, I learned about the expedited trip to the spa. Isn't it bad that it still fell during the school term? Not in the holidays? I am so sorry that I didn't make it in time—"

"Let that be," he interrupted her softly, "—I will tell you everything later—later."

Ruth turned her head to him, listening. Something that touched her as foreign rang in his tone. It was just a single resonating tone, but it didn't belong to Erik. He himself seemed strange to her at this moment. He looked unchanged—exactly the same as before—except for the gaze. The gaze was different, uncertain.

Erik let her go a step ahead unnoticed.

As she climbed the steps to the terrace, his eyes followed every movement of her figure. She had grown considerably, but at the same time, her body had developed more womanly. The dark cloth clothing outlined the fine, slender forms.

The fact that Ruth wore her hair up bothered him.

"The knot takes you away from me—I won't tolerate it," he said when entering the hall, and before she realized it, he had deftly pulled the broad tortoiseshell pin from her hair. In thick curly waves, it fell over her shoulders, as it once did.

"Oh no—not—where is the pin?" she asked bewildered and reached for her back.

"In my jacket pocket.—But repeat that again. Well? 'You?' or 'Du?' The letter said once 'Du.' Only once? Or actually—always?" he asked softly.

She blushed, confused.

"You—you—I—"

Still with his hand in her hair, he gently, irresistibly bent her head back so that she had to lift her entire flushed face to him. She involuntarily closed her eyes, shuddering, and yielded to his hand.

Passionately, deeply serious, his eyes searched her features.

"Mine—" he whispered.

And he leaned forward, and his lips kissed her trembling mouth.

Ruth twitched imperceptibly. He immediately released her and opened the door to his study.

"Here your old place awaits you," he said and went to the window.

But she had not followed. Opposite the window, by the stove, she remained standing, her head with the loose hair leaning against the white tiles, her hands clasped behind her. She looked up at the ceiling, with questioning eyes and a dreamy face.

"What is it?" he asked uneasily, "—Ruth!—what is it?"

He longed to embrace her—to kiss her awake. "You love me—you love me! You don't know it yet, but I know it for you! I know it for sure—feel it, see it—that it is there—that your love, the love of a woman, is there!"

But he was silent.

Yes, it was there—and yet he could not act or speak that way without frightening her away. It was there—like the robin on the swaying branch that flew away at his approach. It was there—but he could not grasp it.

Erik looked silently out into the garden for a moment, then sat down in the old leather chair by the window.

"So, you have not really come home, Ruth," he said, "not fully returned to me. Something in you closes itself to me—will not let me in. Not into the most secret corner of your soul. Not into everything. I have become a stranger to you."

Then she moved from the stove and came to him; she sank down to his knees—pale.

"Yes," she said beside herself, "—a stranger—something foreign—I can't understand it, and it torments me."

"What is it? Tell me."

"I can't," she murmured.

"Yes, yes! You can. Must learn again to speak—or even just stammer—from the innermost—from the most unclear, most misunderstood—. It is only shyness. Overcome it."

"It is—in the kiss," she said softly.

"Did it hurt you—that I kissed you?"

"Hurt me?! Hurt me?! No!—what does it matter to me?"

"—For me—everything, Ruth.—But why does it torment you then?"

She buried her face in her hands.

"—Because—it is the same as in the letter, only in this one—as if it didn't come from you at all—and then: when I spoke of your wife in the garden—and then: in the kiss—I felt it very clearly, the foreignness in it, and that it—"

"That it—?"

"That it shouldn't be," Ruth whispered, "because it is as if it isn't you. A stranger. A worse one."

He did not answer.

When she looked up, timid, questioning, he had closed his eyes.

After a pause, he said in a muffled voice: "You are mistaken. It is nothing foreign—nothing bad. It is me—and in you—it is too—you just don't recognize it—with your childlike eyes."

He stroked her hair and looked away over her, who had bowed her head under his hand.

"Do you remember—when you were here for the first time—what we talked about at this place and what I promised you? I wanted to lead you out of the world of fantasy, where you dreamed, into the world of real life. That happened then, Ruth, and you are no longer the child who dreams, but a fully awakened person who lives—lives with all his young strengths. But do you know how that succeeded? How I could determine and develop you so entirely in your whole being? Only because there was a single point where all the expelled dream spirits, all the silenced fairy tales, all the powers of the enchanting and poetic fantasy fled. That point was your relationship to me. There your gaze did not go to reality, but far beyond every reality to everything that is worthy of worship to a child's heart. There you lived and obeyed not a human, but an image elevated above all humans in your inner self. But this whole dream beauty, Ruth, in which your relationship to me still stands—it is only a shining, radiant form, a childlike covering—not the essence. In it sleeps, like in a fairy tale, the unknown reality and humanity waiting to awaken. Awaken from the dream to life, like your whole remaining being."

He broke off.

She looked up attentively and seriously, trying to follow his words precisely.

"Your beautiful fairy tales," he continued after a short pause, "I had to shatter because they held back your full life. That did not hurt much, for they were only in your head. If I now have to destroy the fantasy world that is intertwined with your whole heart—and cause you pain—will you keep your trust, Ruth—your love—for me?"

She tried to stand up; a feeling of fear suddenly overcame her. He held her back.

"Listen to me, Ruth. If I now told you: the letter, that it sounded foreign to you, was because I myself was in doubt and conflict and fear;—that I kissed you was because I was thirsty for happiness and could no longer do without my happiness;—that I could not bear to hear you speak of my wife was because—I no longer have a wife—because she will separate from me."

"No!" said Ruth breathlessly, "I would not believe that. Not believe it, even if you told me—. Never can that be. Cannot be. Because she—she was so happy—with you."

"She?!" he replied heavily, "—yes, Ruth,—she probably was—earlier. Not because of her must it be. Because of me. Because of you."

Ruth had slowly risen. Her face showed boundless bewilderment—doubt, disbelief, even horror. She felt as if she had to call out to a distant—call to Erik for help against an unknown, misunderstood stranger. But he—it was him standing before her—

Erik saw the change in her features, the self-control left him. He felt only fear—the fear of losing her.

"Ruth!" he cried, "forgive me for you kneeling before me. I will do it before you. Just be mine! No longer just my child—you are no longer a child—a woman—my woman!"

At that moment, the door from the hall was flung open. Jonas appeared on the threshold. He did not enter. He slammed the door again. One could hear him leave.

"Jonas!" Ruth murmured half unconsciously, "—we must—we must see to Jonas."

As she said it, a dull thud sounded. Erik jumped up. Ruth was already at the door. She opened it.

In the hall lay Jonas on the floor—stretched out. He had hit his head against the coat rack when he fell. Blood dripped from his left temple.

Ruth pushed open the middle door. She helped Erik carry him into the adjoining room to his bed. In the next few minutes, they spoke no word. They were silently busy with him.

"The wound is minor," Erik said softly after a short while, and then, bent over him, "He is coming to."

Ruth started. She stepped back from the bed, her eyes fixed on Jonas with an expression of horror, that he might recognize her—that he might see her.

She made a silent sign to Erik and quietly returned to his study.

There she stood, confused.

Here? She could stay even less here. Where then? Nowhere could she stay, nowhere. Not in the whole house. She had to leave. Leave before Erik came. Leave before Jonas came.

And instinctively, she turned again to the door through which she had just entered from the bedrooms.

No, where to? She couldn't go there! Say goodbye? To whom? She had to leave without saying goodbye. Secretly. Unnoticed. Forever?

She stepped into the hall again, as if driven out by her own confused thoughts. There she stopped hesitantly again.

On the floor where Jonas had hit his head, there were a few small bright red spots. Above it, on the rack, hung Erik's coat.

The wide dark travel coat he wore back then—when she was supposed to leave—and he returned—and she fell into his arms—

Ruth stood and stared at the coat. With a pounding heart and held breath.

And suddenly it awoke in her and tore all her thoughts away—wild, glowing, unbearable—the pain of separation.

With her hands, she grabbed the coat, she buried her face in its loose soft folds, with closed eyes she breathed in the faint scent that reminded her of Erik, with trembling lips she kissed the hem.

Back then—if he had commanded her to follow him wherever, for whatever—to death, to crime—would she not have done it blindly?

She clenched her teeth; she groaned, and it seemed to her as if she had to scream out loud.

Oh God, even now—if he had commanded her to follow him wherever, for whatever—she would have done it blindly! Blindly obeying—against all appearances, against all own knowledge and understanding! With her, he could do what he wanted. Whatever happened to her through him—what did it matter to her? But he had to stay up there where she had seen him—his life and his house had to remain what they had been—everything depended on him!

Was it still Erik?

She saw him before her as if in the distant past, as he stood in the midday sunshine last May, bathed in light, the sick wife in his strong arms. That is how Ruth had first seen him with her—that is how she loved and worshiped him, so much that even pity vanished. "You too light a burden!" he joked, and Klare-Bel laughed along and trustingly wrapped her hands around his neck.

But now—now he tore her hands from his neck, and the happy, trusting laughter fell silent—and she, who had held on to him, he let fall—he opened his arms and let her, the helpless one, fall to the ground—for she was a burden, a too heavy burden for his strength. Free had to be his arms, which spread out for Ruth.

•

Ruth straightened up, brushed the hair from her face, and crept slowly back into Erik's study. On the desk lay a pile of white blank sheets. She bent over them and began to write. "I must leave!" it screamed within her. But Erik's pencil formed the letters quite differently. So it came out: "I am not leaving. I go and remain your child."

She looked down at the trembling pencil strokes as if they were a foreign script. So that is what she wanted to do? Yes, that is what she wanted. He had said today that it was all only in her imagination, in her fantasy, that she felt like his child—so completely as his child. But it could still become a reality. If she herself realized it. In her whole future life. If she completely became what he taught her, what he intended with her when he took her in. A piece of him, a work of him. She had everything from him—only from him alone. She knew all his thoughts, all his best. They should become alive, not just dreamed: lived. By her for him.

Ruth took the paper from the desk and placed it on the armchair.

But despite these bold intentions, she did not feel bold at all, but miserable and helpless. She had a single nameless longing: to throw herself on the floor and cry. To cry Erik to her.

But then she heard his voice in her heart—his insistent, persuasive tone: "Hold firm to your own will! Discipline! Obey yourself—do you hear?"

That was indeed strange. More clearly, more surely, more essentially than ever, he stood with her: Erik against Erik.

Quietly she crept out of the house.

Only at the garden gate did she stop and look back.

No, he could not help it, Erik could not help being different, and life being different from what she had imagined. In real life, there were not her fantasy stories. One had to add them.

And had she not dreamed all this, the entire past year? As she stood in the sunshine and bird song, it might seem to her as if she had returned to last May when she leaned here at the gate, anxious and alone, poor and lonely, and looked into the garden. Back then, she thought: from here the spring emanates, the whole beautiful one that bloomed outside. And she dreamed herself a fairy tale, "the most beautiful of all."

Yes, the most beautiful of all.

So beautiful that she could never forget it again. No, never.

So beautiful that she could never give it up for anything else life offered. Never.

So beautiful that there could never be anything—nothing in the whole world—that she would not always measure against it, always compare with it, and find too little.

•

Ruth opened the creaking gate and stepped out onto the road. Without even knowing it, she lifted her hand and gently stroked the bare hard lilac branches that surrounded the fence in a dense thicket.

Then she walked away, without turning back again, with her head bowed, along the country road between the birches to the station, and her long loose childlike hair fluttered in the spring wind.

Erik was still at Jonas's bed. Jonas had opened his eyes, saw his father beside him, started, and closed his eyes again. Not a word was exchanged between them.

Erik now understood the whole context, understood much for which he should have had understanding earlier if he had had thoughts to spare for it. The breathless diligence of Jonas, his eagerness for independence, even in the narrowest life, this tinge of philistinism, this turning away from all joyful recklessness and foolishness now made sense to Erik. Not a lack of temperament, of youthful fire, was it, but iron endurance, self-control.

Childishness or not—there was strength in it. He respected his boy.

But he—the boy—did not respect him.

Not now, in this hour. A whole new relationship with his son, a whole new struggle awaited Erik now, and he had to gather all his strength from now on to win in it.

A faint creaking of the garden gate woke him from these thoughts. At the barely audible sound, a sudden fright flashed through him.

He opened the door to his study. Ruth was not in it. He went through the hall into the living room. Ruth was not there.

Erik went down into the garden. A terrible oppression tightened his chest.

"Ruth!" he called loudly and did not recognize his own voice.

Everything remained still. It remained still, no matter how far he went in, to the bench in front of the grove.

Only a robin sat on the birch branch above the bench and sang.

It wasn't even scared by the footsteps: it sat there completely motionless, with its head raised, completely oblivious—and sang and sang into the gray spring.

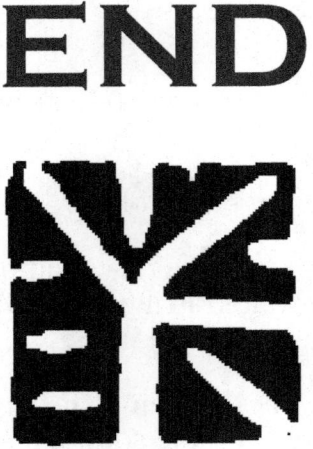